THE USBORNE ILLUSTRATED
ATLAS OF THE
20ᵗʰ CENTURY

LISA MILES AND MANDY ROSS

DESIGNED BY RUTH RUSSELL

ILLUSTRATED BY KUO KANG CHEN, GUY SMITH,
KEVIN JONES ASSOCIATES AND JOHN LAWRENCE

COVER DESIGN BY RUSSELL PUNTER
COVER ILLUSTRATION BY MARK FRANKLIN

CONSULTANTS
ANNE MILLARD, GRAHAM ROBERTS
AND CHRISTOPHER SMITH

CONTENTS

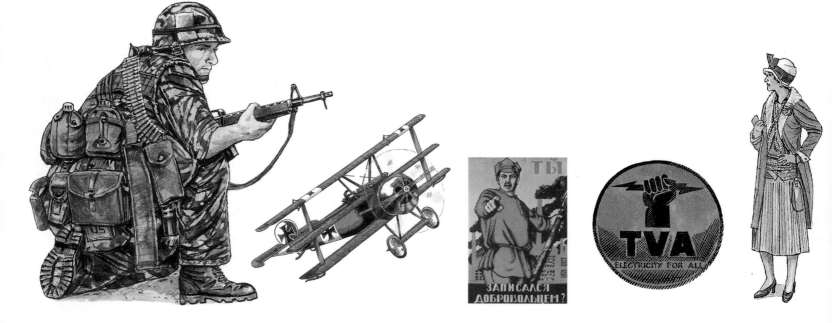

THE TWENTIETH CENTURY

The twentieth century has been a time of great change and conflict. In its early years, the powerful empires of Britain and France were still expanding, while Germany and Italy had also begun to take control of territories abroad. European countries dominated the world. But conflicts within Europe were later to cause two world wars, more terrible than any other war before them.

THE POST-WAR WORLD

In the years after World War Two, the empires were broken up, creating independent nations in Asia and Africa. The new, post-war world was dominated by a period of tension between the great superpowers, the United States of America and the Soviet Union. In the late 1980s, this tension was eased and the mighty Soviet Union was broken up.

THE WORLD TODAY

There are around 180 nation states in the world today. The situation, though, is ever-changing, as national and international conflicts continually alter the political map of the world.

THE EARLY YEARS

In the first years of the twentieth century, European nations competed to establish colonies around the world. As the struggle for land continued, Europeans fought Europeans, and settlers fought native peoples for supremacy.

The Queen's South Africa medal, awarded to British soldiers who fought in the Boer War.

British drummer boy from the Boer War, writing a letter home.

THE BRITISH AND THE BOERS

In southern Africa in 1899, a war broke out between the British and the Boers. The Boers were descendants of Dutch farmers who had colonized southern Africa in the mid-seventeenth century. The Boer War was fiercely fought. Boer guerillas inflicted heavy casualties on British troops, while the British burned Boer farms and herded women and children into camps. The war ended in 1902, when the Boers asked for peace. A new state, the Union of South Africa, was set up in order to reconcile the two sides.

MOROCCAN CRISIS

At this time, France controlled Algeria and Tunisia, and was trying to extend its influence in Morocco too, where Germany also wanted to gain influence. To provoke France, in 1905 the German Kaiser referred in a speech to the Sultan of Morocco as an independent ruler. He was implying that France had no right to interfere in Morocco's affairs. To further provoke France, in 1911, Germany sent a gunboat to the port of Agadir to pressurize Morocco. This tense situation became known as the Agadir Incident.

HERERO REBELLION

By 1900, almost all of Africa had been colonized by European nations. Native peoples often lost their land and were forced to accept European rule. In German Southwest Africa, the Herero people became angry at the loss of their grazing lands and water sources to German settlers.

In 1904, their anger turned into violence and they massacred 123 German colonists. Despite the fact that the Herero had only spears and clubs, it took 14,000 German troops armed with guns to crush the rebellion. They drove 5,000 Herero people into the desert in reprisal. This act of cruelty caused an outcry in Germany.

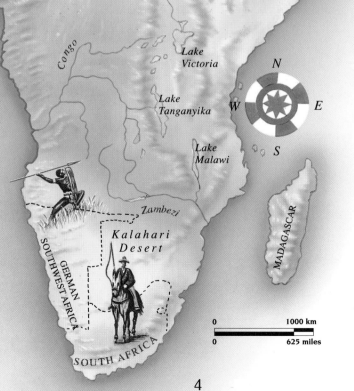

AFRICA

Some areas of conflict in Africa – Morocco, German Southwest Africa and South Africa.

GERMAN SOUTHWEST AFRICA

HERERO TERRITORY

The Herero homeland in German Southwest Africa.

Mediterranean Sea

Agadir •

MOROCCO

TUNISIA

ALGERIA

Sahara Desert

Niger

A F R I C A

Nile

Atlantic Ocean

Congo

Lake Victoria

Lake Tanganyika

Lake Malawi

N
W   E
S

Zambezi

Kalahari Desert

GERMAN SOUTHWEST AFRICA

MADAGASCAR

0   1000 km
0   625 miles

SOUTH AFRICA

THE RUSSO-JAPANESE WAR

The Russian fleet sailed 29,000km (18,000 miles) from the Baltic Sea to fight Japan.

In the early twentieth century, Japan was modernizing. It fought a war with Russia in 1904 because they both had plans to annex (take control of) Manchuria and Korea.

Russia suffered a series of defeats, including the Battle of Mukden and the loss of its fleet at Tsushima. This was a serious blow to the Russians who had sailed their fleet almost all the way around the world to fight Japan.

After the war, Japan gained more territory and also influence over Korea.

FACT BOX

PARIS EXHIBITION

The twentieth century was heralded by an international exhibition held in Paris in 1900. The French President opened the exhibition with a plea for world peace. Little did he know that this new century was to see two world wars more terrible than any other.

THE DOMINIONS

In 1901, the Australian colonies united and became a Dominion of the British Empire; that is, Australia achieved self-rule although it remained part of the empire. Canada had already achieved self-rule in 1867.

New Zealand became a Dominion of the British Empire in 1907.

South Africa became a Dominion of the British Empire in 1910.

SCANDINAVIA

In 1905, the union between Norway and Sweden that began in 1814 ended after demands by Norwegian nationalists. Norway once again became a fully independent country.

THE ARMS RACE

During this period, European nations became great rivals, Germany and Britain in particular. An arms race began in which both countries built up their navies and armed forces.

THE OTTOMAN EMPIRE

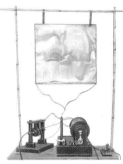

Enver Pasha, Young Turks' leader. He helped to forge closer links with Germany.

During the nineteenth century, the Turkish Ottoman Empire slowly lost its grip on its European provinces and became known as the "sick man of Europe". In the early years of the twentieth century, there was a surge of nationalism – a feeling of patriotism and a desire to bring the Turkish people together. In 1908, the nationalists, called the Young Turks, seized power. Immediately, however, the empire began to lose territory.

In 1908 Bulgaria declared full independence and the Austro-Hungarian Empire annexed Bosnia.

THE BALKAN WARS

Balkan countries at the outbreak of the first Balkan War in October 1912.

More troubles followed with the outbreak of the Balkan Wars in 1912. Serbia, Bulgaria, Greece and Montenegro banded together to expel the Turks from Europe. Within a month they had pushed the Turks back to Constantinople. Albania, too, gained independence. Then in 1913, war broke out again. Serbia and Greece fought Bulgaria for control of territory in the area. Serbia won and became the major power in the Balkans.

The Balkans in 1914. Serbia had enlarged its territory and now it was the major power.

TRAVEL AND COMMUNICATION

During this era, there were many developments in transportation and communication that were to have a huge effect on the twentieth century. In the USA in 1903, Orville Wright made the first flight in a plane. From then on the power, size and safety of planes developed rapidly. In 1908 the motor car became more popular when Ford began to mass-produce the Model-T. Then in 1914 the Panama Canal opened, cutting out the long route for ships around South America.

See above pages for more information.

The Marconiphone, patented in 1896, for sending radio messages.

Communication improved with the development of the telegraph and the telephone. In 1901 Marconi sent the first radio signals across the Atlantic Ocean. In 1911, radio messages helped to bring the English murderer Dr. Crippen to justice. He was escaping on a ship to Canada, but the crew received a signal that he was on board.

Henry Ford's Model-T car. Mass production made the car much cheaper and more available to ordinary people. At first, the Model-T was manufactured in black only. In later years, other paintwork was used.

By 1920, half the cars in the world were Model-T Fords.

WORLD WAR ONE

World War One, also known as the Great War, involved more nations and killed more soldiers than any other war that had been fought before. At first people believed that the war would be over quickly, but it dragged on for four destructive years.

A British wartime poster, encouraging men to enlist in the army or "join up".

Archduke Franz Ferdinand, the heir to the throne of the Austro-Hungarian Empire, who was shot dead.

THE FLASH POINT

The flash point which triggered the war happened in June 1914. Austria had annexed nearby Bosnia, but Serbia wanted to control Bosnia too. On June 28 the heir to the Austro-Hungarian throne and his wife were on a visit to Sarajevo, the Bosnian capital. While driving in an open car through the streets, they were shot dead by a Serbian nationalist. The Austrian government wrongly blamed the Serbian government for the killing. Diplomats tried to ease the tense situation but on July 28, Austria declared war on Serbia. Stability in Europe was now shattered beyond repair. Russia backed Serbia, while Germany supported Austria.

HOW DID IT HAPPEN?

The killing of the Archduke was the immediate cause of the war, but there were deeper causes that had been building up for some time. There were intense trade rivalries between the European nations. Germany was also jealous of Britain, France and others who had acquired colonies abroad. These tensions led to alliances being formed. Britain, France and Russia had drawn together on one side. Germany and Austria were on the other. It was now impossible to prevent all sides from declaring war.

Bosnia and Herzegovina in 1914. It was in Sarajevo, the capital city, that Archduke Franz Ferdinand and his wife were shot.

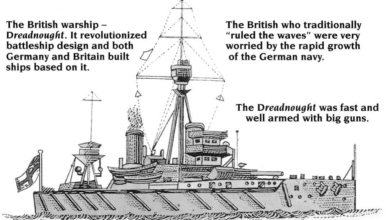

The British warship – *Dreadnought*. It revolutionized battleship design and both Germany and Britain built ships based on it.

The British who traditionally "ruled the waves" were very worried by the rapid growth of the German navy.

The *Dreadnought* was fast and well armed with big guns.

Europe was now split into two camps – the Central Powers (Austria and Germany), versus the Allies (Britain, France and Russia).

THE WESTERN FRONT

As soon as war was declared, the Germans attacked. The plan was to make a dash through neutral Belgium, and inflict a quick defeat on their old enemy France. Then, they planned to turn around and attack Russia. This idea very nearly succeeded, but the Battle of the Marne halted their advance 80km (50 miles) from Paris. Their advance to the north was also stopped by the Allies at the Battle of Ypres, which prevented them from reaching the ports on the coast of the English Channel.

After that, the war became a stalemate across Belgium and northeast France. This area, known as the Western Front, was crisscrossed by a network of trenches, protected by lines of barbed wire.

The German route of attack. It was based on the Schlieffen Plan, which had been devised as early as 1905 in readiness for any war that might break out with France.

The Western Front. Trenches were dug across northern France to Switzerland. After autumn 1914, the frontline hardly moved until the end of the war.

NEW WEAPONS

To gain the upper hand, both sides used new weapons, such as poison gas and tanks. Another major development was the use of aircraft. Planes were first used to find out what was happening behind enemy lines (called reconnaissance). They were later used as fighters. During the war, the British Sopwith Camel shot down more planes than any other fighter.

This plane is the Fokker Dr-1, flown by the German fighter ace, Manfred von Richthofen. He was known as the Red Baron, after his red plane.

TRENCH WARFARE

Soldiers lived in appalling conditions in the muddy trenches. They were wet, cold and bombarded by gunfire. They suffered this miserable existence for months on end. The order to attack, or "go over the top", might win an advance of only a short distance, with the loss of perhaps thousands of men. Due to the heavy casualties, men were conscripted (ordered to join the forces). In Britain, men between 18 and 41 were made to join up.

FACT BOX

THE ALLIES

The Allies were Britain, France, Russia, Japan and Serbia. They were later joined by Italy (1915), Portugal and Romania (1916), and the USA and Greece (1917).

THE CENTRAL POWERS

The Central Powers were Germany, the Austro-Hungarian Empire and Turkey. They were later joined by Bulgaria (1915).

CHRISTMAS DAY 1914

On this day, German and British troops made an informal ceasefire. They sang Christmas carols to each other from their own positions and met in no-man's land between the trenches, to exchange photographs and gifts as souvenirs. Some soldiers played games of football together in no-man's land.

FIND OUT MORE

Serbia	☞	5
World War One	☞	8

See above pages for more information.

BAPAUME

After five months of fighting, the Allies managed to advance only 10km (6 miles).

GERMAN TERRITORY

Shell fire churned the ground up so that it was nearly impossible to advance.

ALBERT

ALLIED TERRITORY

This battle was the first in which tanks were used.

Over 600,000 Allies and 650,000 Germans were killed in the battle.

PERONNE

Somme

BATTLE OF THE SOMME

One of the most famous battles of the war was the Battle of the Somme. It took place between July and November 1916.

BRITAIN

BELGIUM

Battle of the Somme

FRANCE

Paris

KEY

Frontline July 1916

Frontline November 1916

THE WIDER WAR

T. E. Lawrence, known as Lawrence of Arabia.

As World War One settled into a stalemate on the Western Front, fighting broke out in other regions. In the west, the Germans had failed to defeat France as planned, and were faced with the task of fighting Russia in the east at the same time.

A soldier from the Australia and New Zealand Army Corps (ANZAC), which fought at Gallipoli.

THE EASTERN FRONT

The Russians, though brave fighters, were ill-prepared for war. They were badly equipped and they suffered several defeats with heavy casualties. Poverty plagued the Russian people and by 1917 they were deeply unhappy with their leader, Czar Nicholas II. A revolution broke out, forcing the Czar to abdicate. A new Russian government eventually made peace with Germany.

The Eastern Front in 1915. The Russians and the Poles had attacked first, but the Germans drove them back.

THE ARAB REVOLT

Arabia had been dominated by the Ottoman Empire for many years. The Sharif of Mecca, Hussein ibn Ali, now took his chance and rose in revolt. His son, the Emir Feisal, worked with the British officer T. E. Lawrence to combine their forces against the Turks. From 1916, the Arabs kept in close contact with the British army. In 1918, they entered Damascus together – victorious.

Arabia and the Ottoman Empire in 1914. The empire had been weakening for many years and the Arabs wanted independence.

GALLIPOLI

For the Allies, the defeat of the Turkish Ottoman Empire would open routes through the Black Sea to Russia, India, and the oil wells in Persia. In 1915, they invaded the Gallipoli peninsula on the Turkish coast.

The attack was badly planned and the Turks held strong positions above the beaches. Allied troops, many from the Australia and New Zealand Army Corps (ANZAC), endured eight months of fighting, gaining nothing. Many lives were lost and Allied forces were eventually evacuated.

THE INVASION

This map shows the Gallipoli peninsula. The Allies tried to force their way through the Dardanelles by ship, but when that failed, troops were landed on the beaches. The invasion was a terrible failure.

BULGARIA
GREECE
Gallipoli
OTTOMAN EMPIRE
AEGEAN SEA

Imbroz

Aegean Sea

Suvla Bay

Turkish positions

Anzac Cove

The tiny beach assaulted by the ANZAC forces was nicknamed Anzac Cove.

Turkish positions

Cape Helles

Gallipoli

GALLIPOLI

Dardanelles

ÇANAKKALE

TURKEY

The Dardanelles channel leads from the Aegean Sea to the Black Sea, and so to Russia.

KEY

➤ Allied invasion

★ Battle

• Turkish mines

N W E S

WAR AT SEA

The main sea battle took place at Jutland in 1916. There was no winner.

The battleships of Britain and Germany did not play such a big role in the war as expected. Instead, Germany used submarines to attack supply ships, and very nearly starved Britain. In 1915, the Germans sank two passenger ships, the *Lusitania* and the *Arabia*, with great loss of life. This later helped to persuade the USA to enter the war against Germany.

German submarines (U-boats) attacked Allied shipping around Europe.

FACT BOX

CASUALTY FIGURES
Gallipoli, 1915

25,000 Allied troops dead
76,000 wounded
13,000 missing.

Total deaths 1914-1918

British Empire 947,000
France 1,375,000
Italy 460,000
USA 115,600
Russia* 1,700,000
Germany 1,808,500
Ottoman Empire* 325,000
Austro-Hungarian
  Empire* 1,200,000

*These figures may be inaccurate and are likely to be much higher.

**T. E. LAWRENCE
(1888-1935)**

Lawrence of Arabia, as he was known, studied the Middle East at Oxford University. In 1916, he went to Arabia to help the Emir in his revolt against the Turks, Germany's allies.

After the war, he became a special adviser on Arab affairs to the British government. He felt that the Arab cause was betrayed when control over the area was given to Britain and France.

WOMEN'S ROLES

Edith Cavell, a British nurse, was executed by the Germans for helping Allied prisoners to escape.

While their menfolk were away fighting on the frontline, many women occupied roles traditionally filled by men. At home they took on jobs such as working in arms factories and driving buses.

Some became involved in the actual war, serving as ambulance drivers and nurses. A few took on more daring roles. They became spies and resistance fighters, working behind enemy lines.

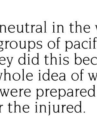

The Dutch dancer, known as Mata Hari. She was executed by the British for being a German spy.

PACIFISTS

Few countries managed to stay neutral in the war. Within some countries, however, were groups of pacifists who refused to fight on principle. They did this because they disagreed so strongly with the whole idea of warfare, for whatever cause. Some pacifists were prepared to act on the frontline as stretcher-bearers for the injured.

Pacifist societies used emblems such as this one. The dove represents peace.

FIND OUT MORE

Russian
Revolution ☞ 10

Peace
treaties ☞ 12

See above pages for more information.

THE USA ENTERS THE WAR

In April 1917, the USA declared war on Germany. Submarine warfare had killed many of its citizens and Americans rallied behind the Allies. By now Allied forces were weak, so fresh troops and equipment were valuable. With so many men and resources against them, defeat for Germany was certain.

THE END AT LAST

The Allies gained control of the sea and Germany grew short of food and raw materials. One by one, the Central Powers surrendered. The guns finally fell silent on November 11, 1918. At least ten million people died in World War One. It is possible that this figure may be much higher as some records are inadequate. Peace treaties were made separately with each of the Central Powers. There were enormous problems to solve and the suffering left many feeling very bitter.

For the people of the Allied nations, the end of the war was a joyous celebration. These people took to the streets on Armistice Day – November 11, 1918.

RUSSIAN REVOLUTION

Czar Nicholas II, with his family. They were murdered in 1918, in the aftermath of the revolution.

As the twentieth century dawned, Czar Nicholas II ruled one-sixth of the Earth's surface. The Russian Empire was vast, but it had not kept pace with progress in the rest of Europe. Noble families lived in sumptuous palaces, while millions of peasants scratched out a miserable life of hardship.

The Czar's jewel-encrusted crown was a symbol of his immense wealth and power.

CZARIST RUSSIA

The Russian Empire was trying to catch up with European industrial progress. But factory workers and peasants, poor and hungry, were growing restless. A disastrous war against Japan in 1904-5 caused mutiny in the army, and riots at home. In 1905 troops fired at demonstrators at the Czar's Winter Palace. This event sparked a rebellion. In a panic, the Czar set up a new parliament, the Duma. But it had little real power. Whenever it criticized the Czar, he simply closed it down.

WORLD WAR ONE

In 1914 Russia entered World War One. The Czar hoped that war might quieten unrest at home. But the troops were hopelessly ill-prepared. By the end of 1914, a quarter of the army was lost. Although he was no soldier, the Czar himself went off to take charge at the front. Back in Russia, the war caused terrible food and fuel shortages. Women lay on the rails to stop troop trains from leaving. Left in charge, the Czarina and her adviser, Rasputin, grew unpopular. "Revolution!" was whispered everywhere.

FEBRUARY 1917

Tired of waiting in frozen streets for rationed bread, in 1917 the women of Petrograd (now St. Petersburg) sparked off the February Revolution. Millions of factory workers went on strike. Instead of firing on them, troops joined the demonstrators. Czar Nicholas tried to get home, but railway workers stopped his train outside Petrograd. There, in a train siding, he abdicated. The Duma took over, but could neither win the war nor end it. The Czar's fall seemed to change nothing.

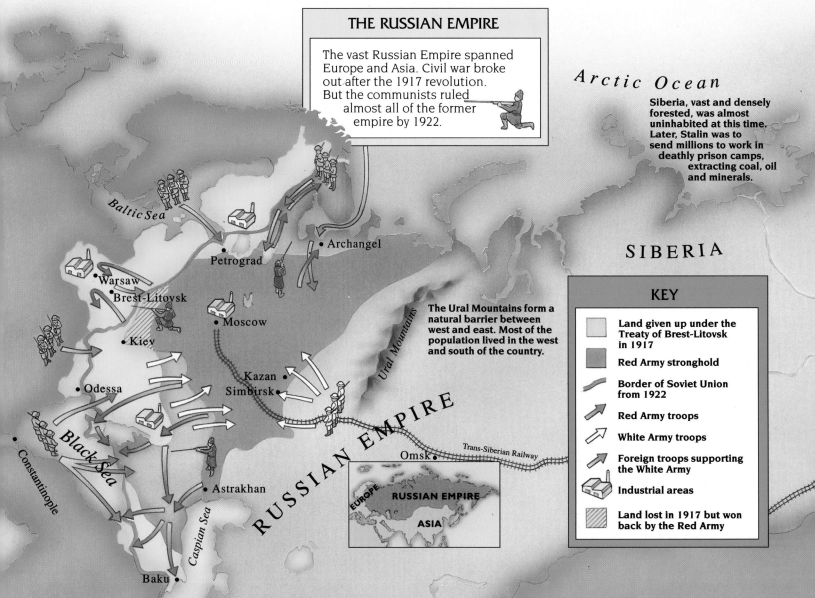

THE RUSSIAN EMPIRE

The vast Russian Empire spanned Europe and Asia. Civil war broke out after the 1917 revolution. But the communists ruled almost all of the former empire by 1922.

Siberia, vast and densely forested, was almost uninhabited at this time. Later, Stalin was to send millions to work in deathly prison camps, extracting coal, oil and minerals.

The Ural Mountains form a natural barrier between west and east. Most of the population lived in the west and south of the country.

Arctic Ocean

SIBERIA

Baltic Sea

Archangel

Petrograd

Warsaw

Brest-Litovsk

Moscow

Kiev

Kazan

Odessa

Simbirsk

Ural Mountains

Black Sea

Constantinople

Astrakhan

Caspian Sea

Baku

RUSSIAN EMPIRE

Omsk

Trans-Siberian Railway

EUROPE

RUSSIAN EMPIRE

ASIA

KEY

Land given up under the Treaty of Brest-Litovsk in 1917

Red Army stronghold

Border of Soviet Union from 1922

Red Army troops

White Army troops

Foreign troops supporting the White Army

Industrial areas

Land lost in 1917 but won back by the Red Army

PEACE! BREAD! LAND!

The Bolsheviks, followers of Karl Marx's communist teachings, wanted to create a socialist society. All men and women would be equal. Wealth was to be shared, putting an end to poverty and injustice. With their slogan "Peace! Bread! Land!", the Bolsheviks won support among the war-weary, hungry people. In April 1917 the Bolshevik leader, Vladimir Il'yich Ulianov, known as Lenin, returned from exile. Under his leadership, the Bolsheviks' power grew rapidly.

Communism offered real change to peasants, like these women hauling a barge.

BOLSHEVIK REVOLUTION

In the small hours of October 25, 1917, groups of Bolsheviks quietly occupied Petrograd's railway stations, telephone exchanges and post office. At 2am they stormed the Winter Palace, arrested the Duma, and declared a new revolutionary government. Hardly a drop of blood was shed.

Lenin's first act, as he had promised, was to bring Russia out of the war. Then – because he needed the peasants' support – he ordered the nobles' land to be shared among the people. This won the Bolsheviks huge popularity.

Petrograd's landmarks, seized by the Bolsheviks.

CIVIL WAR

There was an immediate backlash from the Czar's supporters, nobles and liberals, who formed the White Army. Foreign countries sent massive support to try to stop communism from spreading. By the summer of 1918, a murderous civil war raged throughout the old Czarist Empire.

By the spring of 1919, the Bolsheviks' newly-formed Red Army had begun to turn the tide. But the fighting dragged on, followed in 1921 by a catastrophic drought and famine. Millions died of hunger and thirst. There were even reports of cannibalism.

This Bolshevik propaganda poster asks "Have you joined the Red Army?"

FIND OUT MORE

Russo-Japanese War	☞	5
World War One	☞	6
Stalin's Soviet Union	☞	20

See above pages for more information.

BIRTH OF THE SOVIET UNION

By 1922, the Communists (the Bolsheviks' new name) had won the civil war. But the economy was in ruins. Lenin encouraged people to buy and sell freely. Soon the markets were full of food and goods.

The mid-1920s was a hopeful, exciting time in the Soviet Union (as the nation was renamed). Education was free to all. The revolution was celebrated with art, music and film. Women welcomed their new rights, such as education and divorce.

But the Communists' state police force, the Cheka, dealt ruthlessly with anyone who disagreed with the government. The seeds were sown for the reign of terror under the next Soviet leader, Stalin.

The Communist Party symbol, the hammer and sickle, decorated all kinds of objects, like this hand-painted plate.

Sea of Okhotsk

During the civil war, foreign troops came from the east to support the White Army. They came on the Trans-Siberian railway.

JAPAN

Vladivostock

PEACE AFTER WAR

After the war German weapons, such as tanks, were broken up.

At the end of World War One, international conferences were held to decide the peace settlements. The settlements were to state what should happen to the countries involved in the war – especially the losers.

War memorials were built after the war to commemorate those who died.

THE TREATY OF VERSAILLES

In 1919 at the Palace of Versailles near Paris, a conference was held to make a settlement between Germany and the Allies. A treaty was signed by 27 nations, of which 17 were non-European. Also at the conference, an organization called the League of Nations was set up to try to prevent war in future. The failure of the USA and the Soviet Union to join the League, however, made it weak. Separate treaties followed with Germany's allies.

British children celebrating the Versailles Peace Treaty with a tea party.

GERMANY'S FATE

A German stamp valued at 5,000 million marks.

The main outcome of the Treaty of Versailles was that Germany was made to admit its guilt and to take full responsiblity for causing World War One. It was made to agree to enormous sums as reparations – financial payments to the Allies. Germany also had to reduce its army and navy drastically, and was not allowed tanks or submarines.

It also had to give up land to its former enemies. The colonies were handed to the Allies as mandates – regions that the Allies should rule for the time being until they could be given independence. Germany found it impossible to pay the reparations and the value of its currency fell. Before long, the value of the German mark sank to 10,000 million for £1 and 48,000 million for $1.

NEW COUNTRIES

Separate treaties were made with the old Austro-Hungarian Empire and the Ottoman Empire, which were both broken up. A separate treaty was also made with their ally Bulgaria. The map of Europe was now redrawn in order to give independence to nations that had previously been part of the old empires. Several of these new countries, however, contained two or more different nationalities and also different religious groups.

For instance, a third of Poland's population did not speak Polish. Among its new inhabitants were Russian and German speakers. This problem made many of the new countries unstable, as the different cultural groups vied with each other for dominance within the new nations.

The flag of Poland – one of the new countries in 1919.

After the treaty, Germany had to give up territory. The Rhineland was to be occupied by Allied troops for 15 years and no German troops were ever to be stationed there.

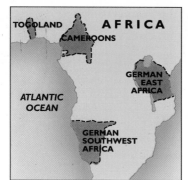

German Southwest Africa became a South African mandate and German East Africa became a British one. The Cameroons and Togoland were divided between Britain and France.

Europe after the peace treaties. Germany and the Austro-Hungarian and Ottoman Empires were broken up and new countries in central Europe came into being. In addition, although not part of the treaties, Finland became independent from Russia in 1917 and the Irish Free State (formally part of Britain) was created in 1921.

THE MIDDLE EAST

The former Middle East territories of the Ottoman Empire either became mandates or gained independence. During the 1920s and 30s, there was an increasing worldwide demand for oil as motor transportation took over and the use of oil in industry increased. The huge amounts of oil that were being discovered in the Middle East made it very valuable territory.

From 1935, Persia was known as Iran.

In 1925, the Shah of Persia was overthrown. Colonel Reza Khan was elected Shah and modernized Persia, though he grew wealthy at the expense of his country.

Egypt was recognized as independent in 1922 under King Fuad I. British forces were still stationed there.

Saudi Arabia was unified into a single kingdom in 1932. The first oil exports were made in 1938.

Areas under British and French control in Arabia eventually gained full independence during or after World War Two.

KEY

- British control or influence
- French control or influence
- British mandate
- French mandate
- Oil producing areas

| 0 | | 500 | km |
| 0 | 300 | | miles |

THE REPUBLIC OF TURKEY

In 1919 the Turkish Nationalist Movement, led by Mustafa Kemal, called for a Turkish republic. The old Ottoman Empire was abolished and in 1923 the new Republic of Turkey was recognized.

Kemal was its first president. He began reforms to modernize Turkey and he separated the state from religious controls. A new legal system, schools and universities were set up. From 1928 the Latin alphabet was used, not Arabic script. In 1934 Turkish women were given more freedom. They were no longer forced to wear a veil and men were no longer allowed more than one wife.

Kemal took the name Ataturk – "Father of the Turks". He ruled Turkey as a dictator until his death in 1938.

FIND OUT MORE

| Ottoman Empire | ☞ | 5 |
| World War One | ☞ | 6 |

See above pages for more information

THE GREAT DEPRESSION

In the USA, the period after World War One was called the "Era of Big Business". The capitalist economy brought new wealth, as mass production improved and new consumer goods became available. But within ten years, this prosperity vanished. The USA entered a period of poverty that deeply affected the rest of the industrialized world.

The Ku Klux Klan wore white robes and hats and usually masked their faces.

This car was used as a home by a farmer and his family, who left the Midwest to find work in California.

THE KU KLUX KLAN

One of the more sinister aspects of the postwar period was the rise in popularity of a group called the Ku Klux Klan. Founded in 1915, the Klan attacked nonwhites, Jews and Catholics – in fact anyone whose ideas and values they disagreed with.

They terrorized their victims with violence and were particularly active in the 1920s in the south of the United States and also the Midwest.

THE USA

The United States of America in the 1920s and 30s. Dust storms from drought-hit areas blew as far as New York on the east coast.

THE DUSTBOWLS

The 1920s and 30s were troubled times for people in America's farming regions. Farmers felt that their interests were being neglected. They made little money from their produce. Severe droughts caused the land to become very dry. Bad farming practices made the problem worse. In some areas, soil erosion was so bad that farms became giant dustbowls. Many small farmers were ruined and could not support their families.

GANGSTERS

In 1920, the 18th Amendment to the Constitution banned the production and sale of alcohol in the USA. The period during which alcohol was illegal is called the Prohibition. It lasted until 1933. The law was an attempt to stop people from drinking alcohol, but it soon became unpopular. Organized crime flourished as groups of gangsters, such as the Mafia, controlled businesses and alcohol smuggling.

A 1920s gangster and his female accomplice.

KEY

🏙 • Industrial city

Dustbowl

➤ Migrant workers leaving the dustbowl

THE WALL STREET CRASH

October 24, 1929 is known as Black Thursday – the day that the New York Stock Exchange crashed, making stocks and shares virtually worthless. The crash was caused by weaknesses in basic industries, such as agriculture, mining and textiles. Many people were investing money on the stock exchange. Share prices fell suddenly and panic set in. This disaster is called the Wall Street Crash after Wall Street, the home of the New York Stock Exchange.

After the crash, industrial production in the USA fell by over a half. Banks called in their loans and businesses everywhere were ruined. These problems spread worldwide. Around 15 million people in the USA, 6 million in Germany and 3 million in Britain became unemployed. This period of severe poverty is known as the Great Depression. The hardship lasted until 1934, when the economy began to recover at last.

These unemployed men are waiting for free soup, which was handed out to the poor during the Great Depression.

LINE FOR
1¢ RESTAURANT

20 MEALS FOR 1¢
DONATIONS WANTED
HELP FEED THE HUNGRY
1 WILL FEED 20
1¢ RESTAURANT
107 W 43ᴿᴰ ST

THE NEW DEAL

In 1932, Franklin D. Roosevelt was elected President and he announced a series of emergency measures, known as the New Deal, to end the Great Depression. There were plans to help both industry and farming, while public building projects were started to create jobs.

One of these projects was the setting up of the Tennessee Valley Authority. This organization worked on the Tennessee River to improve the irrigation (watering) of the land. It also built power stations to supply energy to new industries, and planted trees to prevent soil erosion.

Symbols against depression – a badge from Roosevelt's Democratic Party (left) and the logo of the Tennessee Valley Authority (right).

FIND OUT MORE

World War One ☞ 6

World War Two ☞ 22

For more information see above pages.

A cartoon dated September 1939, showing the indecision of the American people over whether or not to get involved in World War Two.

ISOLATIONISM

After World War One, many Americans wanted to keep out of European affairs. This idea, which had often been part of American policy, was known as "isolationism". Despite strong opposition, however, President Roosevelt started to establish closer relations with foreign countries. When Europe went to war in 1939, opinions in the USA were split over whether or not to get involved.

HELP THEM!

DO NOTHING!

LAOCOÖN 1938

CHINA AND JAPAN

In the nineteenth century, Japan had begun to modernize. Services, such as schools and the police, were organized along European lines. A parliament was introduced and in 1925 adult men got the vote. China, in contrast, avoided Westernization as much as possible.

Pu-Yi, the last Emperor of China, was deposed in 1912.

THE FALL OF THE EMPEROR

In China, the government of the six-year-old Emperor, Pu-Yi, was becoming increasingly weak and unpopular. In 1911, a revolution broke out. One of the most important revolutionaries was Dr. Sun Yat-sen, founder of the Kuomintang – the National People's Party. His ideas were based on no interference by foreign powers, democracy and a guaranteed income for all. For a short while after the revolution, he became President of the new republic.

Emperor Hirohito of Japan ruled from 1926-1989.

THE WARLORDS

After the revolution, the Nationalist government found it hard to bring its huge country under control. Local military leaders, called the Warlords, set themselves up as rulers in their own districts. They recruited private armies which they used to terrorize peasants and increase their own power and wealth. Civil war followed.

Chiang Kai-shek (1887-1975).

Between 1926 and 1928 the head of the Nationalists, Chiang Kai-shek, led a victorious campaign against the Warlords. He also achieved other improvements, such as the building of roads, railways and some hospitals and factories.

JAPAN BETWEEN THE WARS

While China struggled, the 1920s were troubled times for Japan too. As one of the victors in World War One, it was given German territory in the Pacific Ocean, but there were financial scandals and in 1923 an earthquake devastated Tokyo and Yokohama. Like other industrialized nations, it also suffered during the Great Depression. When Hirohito became Emperor of Japan in 1926, the country was unstable and a spate of political murders in the 1930s made matters worse.

Japan had been trying to influence China for some years. In a bid for colonial power, in 1931 Japan occupied Manchuria (part of China) and renamed it Manchukuo. Pu-Yi, the former Emperor of China, was set up as its head of state under Japanese control.

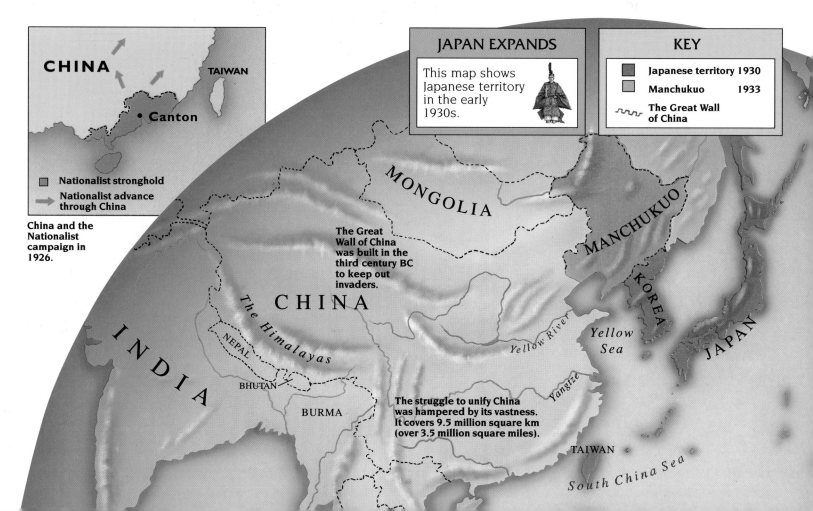

CHINA

TAIWAN

• Canton

☐ Nationalist stronghold
→ Nationalist advance through China

China and the Nationalist campaign in 1926.

JAPAN EXPANDS

This map shows Japanese territory in the early 1930s.

KEY

☐ Japanese territory 1930
☐ Manchukuo 1933
〰 The Great Wall of China

MONGOLIA

The Great Wall of China was built in the third century BC to keep out invaders.

MANCHUKUO

CHINA

KOREA

INDIA

NEPAL

The Himalayas

Yellow River

Yellow Sea

JAPAN

BHUTAN

Yangtze

BURMA

The struggle to unify China was hampered by its vastness. It covers 9.5 million square km (over 3.5 million square miles).

TAIWAN

South China Sea

THE LONG MARCH

Meanwhile the Chinese Communist Party was growing powerful. Originally, it had worked with the Nationalists, but in 1927 it broke away and set up its own government in Kiangsi. In 1934, the Nationalist army encircled the Communists. During this siege up to one million people may have been starved or killed. The communist Red Army escaped by trudging 8,000km (5,000 miles) to Yenan in the north. Out of 100,000 people, only 30,000 survived this journey, called the Long March.

Japan was suspicious of the both the Chinese and the Soviet communists. So, it joined the Anti-Comintern Pact with Germany and Italy in 1936, in order to work against communism.

THE SINO-JAPANESE WAR

In 1937 there was a clash between Chinese troops and the staff of the Japanese Embassy in Beijing. This incident sparked off a full-scale war. Japan invaded China, bombing Chinese cities and occupying important industrial regions near the coast. Troops behaved with appalling cruelty to civilians, looting and killing. The Chinese Nationalist government enlisted the help of the Communists to help fight the invaders, but the Japanese army was too strong. Although the Japanese were unable to occupy the whole country, it was impossible for the Chinese to expel them.

The invasion was condemned by the League of Nations but Japan took no notice. It had been disappointed in the League right from the start because it had failed to include a clause of racial equality in its covenant (agreement). Japan now responded to the League's protests by just resigning from it.

Only the Soviet Union, determined not to lose any of its own territory, stood up to Japan, defeating it at Nomonchau in 1939. In the same year, World War Two broke out, leaving China and Japan to struggle on until 1945.

The Long March, which began in October 1934, took a whole year to complete. The marchers crossed 18 mountain ranges and 24 rivers, fighting skirmishes almost every day. For years after this, the Chinese Communist Party was dominated by its survivors, including Mao Zedong.

Japan's invasion route into China in 1937. Troops swept swiftly down from Manchukuo and captured Beijing. A second force, brought by the Japanese navy, took Shanghai.

Japanese territory in 1938. By this time, Japan had conquered large areas of northern China, including the important industrial areas, such as Canton.

FACT BOX

SUN YAT-SEN (1867-1925)

Born as the son of a Chinese peasant, Sun Yat-Sen was an American citizen for some years and trained as a doctor in Hong Kong. After the Chinese Revolution in 1911, he became President in 1913.

He soon resigned, however, in the interests of unity. He remained a great influence on the government but died of cancer before China could be unified.

HENRY PU-YI (1906-67)

Pu-Yi became the last Manchu Emperor of China in 1908 when he was two years old. After the Chinese Revolution in 1911, he was allowed to live in a palace in Beijing.

Disorder in China caused him to seek safety in Japanese-held territory. The Japanese made him Emperor of Manchukuo in 1934, but he was just a figurehead. In 1945 he was captured by the Soviets and was imprisoned in Siberia. In 1950 he was handed back to China and lived as a private citizen.

THE 21 DEMANDS

As far back as 1915, Japan had been trying to influence China. It demanded a list of concessions from China known as the 21 Demands. They included: Japanese advisors to be employed by the Chinese government; major industries to be put under joint control; police in trade areas to be under joint control; and no bay or island to be leased to any country except Japan.

Japanese troops entering Beijing in 1937.

Pacific Ocean

THE RISE OF FASCISM

Nazi Germany used the eagle as a symbol of strength and nationalism.

The horrors of World War One shattered many of the old certainties in Europe. Empires had fallen, and governments seemed unsure. In many countries, people turned to a new movement, called fascism. Its leaders offered simple answers to problems caused by the war.

WHAT IS FASCISM?

Fascism, which first emerged in Italy, was a new and violent political movement. It appealed to traditional virtues, such as unity, nationalism and love of the motherland. Its leaders – mainly military men – offered strong discipline and demanded absolute obedience to their orders. Fascism quickly gathered strength, spreading across Europe and South America.

Fascism took its name from the bundle of rods, or *fasces*, which symbolized authority in Ancient Rome.

The fascists hated communism, but they also wanted to destroy the old aristocracy. Just like classroom bullies, they built up a feeling of fearful unity by picking scapegoats, and encouraging people to attack them. This combination of ideas appealed to the poor, and also to the middle classes whose comfort and savings were threatened by the chaos of inflation (steep price rises), falling wages and unemployment.

Mussolini, like other fascist dictators, stirred crowds into a frenzy of rage and hatred with his passionate speeches.

ITALY

Following World War One, Italy faced unemployment and soaring prices, despite being on the winning side. People lost faith in the faltering government. Many, especially powerful factory owners and Church leaders, feared a communist takeover.

The time was ripe for Benito Mussolini, a journalist and ex-soldier, to launch the first fascist movement, *fascio di combattimento*, or "fascists for the battle". He promised to smash the threat of communism and make Italy a powerful nation. Many people welcomed his strong leadership.

Mussolini's supporters, black-shirted young thugs, fought on the streets and terrorized politicians. The government was unable to tame them. King Victor Emmanuel III was afraid of a communist revolution, so in 1922 he agreed to make Mussolini prime minister. Gradually Mussolini removed all his enemies and became a dictator.

Hitler adopted the swastika as the Nazi emblem.

GERMANY

The German economy was shattered by World War One. After the New York Stock Exchange crash in 1929, German money became almost worthless. Inflation meant that people needed a suitcase full of cash to buy a loaf of bread. In this climate, a new form of fascism quickly took hold. It was called Nazism, and was built on violent race hatred. The Nazis encouraged anti-Semitism, or hatred of Jews, whom they blamed for all Germany's economic problems.

ADOLF HITLER AND THE NAZIS

Adolf Hitler, a fanatical anti-Semite, had set up the Nazi party in 1920. It grew rapidly. His rabble-rousing speeches offered a vision of a glorious German master race, superior to Jews and dark-skinned peoples. Led by a powerful leader, or *Führer*, they would build a thousand-year empire. Hungry, desperate and still resentful of the terms of the Treaty of Versailles, millions of Germans rallied to Hitler's call.

Elected as chancellor, or head of government, in 1933, Hitler soon removed all other parties from power. He set up vicious prison camps such as Dachau, and on the "Night of the Long Knives", in June 1934, his henchmen murdered over a hundred of his rivals. Nazi thugs attacked German Jews and their homes and shops. Jewish children were expelled from schools. On *Kristallnacht* (Crystal Night) in 1938, hundreds of synagogues were burned down and thousands of Jews were arrested – a grim sign of things to come.

THE SPANISH CIVIL WAR

Isolated and backward, Spain kept out of World War One. In 1931, a new Republican government set out to improve the lives of the poor. But in doing so, they made many powerful enemies.

SPAIN

PORTUGAL

☐ Franco's conquests
☐ Republican areas

Republicans in northern and eastern Spain held out against Franco until 1939.

By 1936, General Franco had united the government's enemies under a fascist banner. Civil war broke out. To support Franco, German planes carried out devastating air raids on Spanish cities. Over 30,000 men from 54 countries joined the Republicans' fight against fascism. But they were no match for Franco's professional army. In 1939 the fascists won. Franco became Spain's dictator until his death in 1975.

In the Spanish Civil War, both sides used propaganda to get their message across. Some was even aimed at children. This doll, with its cut-out uniforms, is making a fascist salute.

DICTATORS IN EUROPE

This map shows how the nations of Europe were governed in 1938. Many countries were in the grip of fascist rulers or other harsh, unelected dictators.

KEY

☐ Fascist dictatorships
☐ Other dictatorships
☐ Democracies
☐ Communist states
↘ Italy's invasion route to Ethiopia

0	500	1000 km
0	300	600 miles

FASCIST AGGRESSION

Having promised their people glory, fascist leaders needed to produce victories to satisfy them.

By the mid-1930s, Mussolini's economic plans were in ruins and the people were growing restless. To distract them, in 1935 he launched an attack on Ethiopia. The Ethiopian Emperor, Haile Selassie, asked for support from the League of Nations. But it failed to stop Mussolini.

Emperor Haile Selassie, ruler of Ethiopia, which was also then known as Abyssinia.

Watching in Germany, Hitler seized the moment. He ordered troops into the Rhineland, although this was forbidden by the Treaty of Versailles. The League of Nations made no response at all.

The Rhineland acted as a buffer between Germany and France.

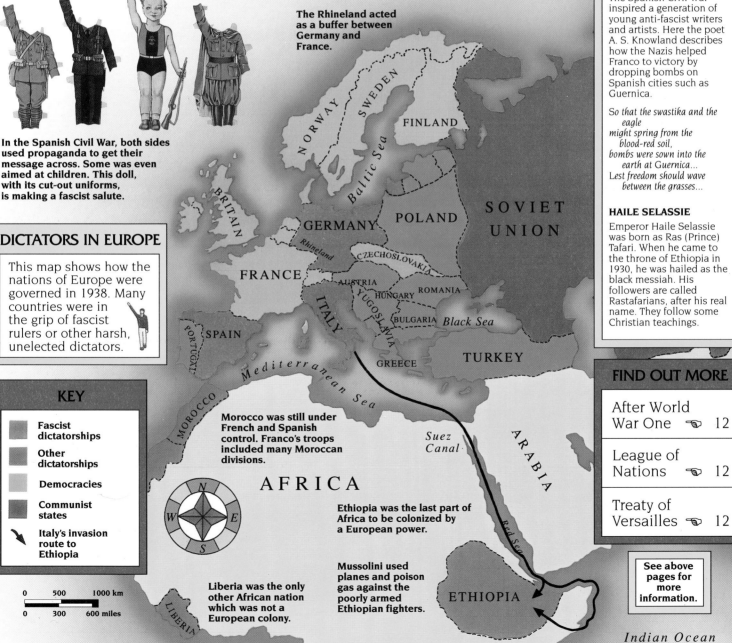

NORWAY
SWEDEN
FINLAND
BRITAIN
Baltic Sea
GERMANY
POLAND
SOVIET UNION
Rhineland
FRANCE
CZECHOSLOVAKIA
AUSTRIA
HUNGARY
ROMANIA
PORTUGAL
SPAIN
ITALY
YUGOSLAVIA
BULGARIA
Black Sea
GREECE
TURKEY
Mediterranean Sea
MOROCCO
Suez Canal
ARABIA
AFRICA
Red Sea
ETHIOPIA
Atlantic Ocean
Indian Ocean

Morocco was still under French and Spanish control. Franco's troops included many Moroccan divisions.

Ethiopia was the last part of Africa to be colonized by a European power.

Liberia was the only other African nation which was not a European colony.

Mussolini used planes and poison gas against the poorly armed Ethiopian fighters.

FIND OUT MORE

After World War One ☞	12
League of Nations ☞	12
Treaty of Versailles ☞	12

See above pages for more information.

STALIN'S SOVIET UNION

Joseph Stalin chose his own name, meaning "man of steel".

By 1924, the civil war and famine that followed the Russian Revolution were over. Communism was starting to succeed. Joseph Stalin emerged as the new leader when Lenin died. He modernized the Soviet Union, transforming it from a backward agricultural nation to an industrial giant and an atomic superpower. But these changes cost immeasurable human suffering.

This propaganda poster shows agricultural workers as heroes.

RISE TO POWER

After Lenin's death, Stalin worked his way to power by encouraging quarrels between his rivals, including Leon Trotsky, Lenin's second in command. By 1929 he was every bit as powerful as the Czar had once been. Stalin was seen as a trusted father figure who would lead the country to peace and plenty. But he was ruthless. He silenced his critics at home and exiled Trotsky, whom he later had assassinated.

THE FIVE YEAR PLANS

"We are fifty or a hundred years behind the advanced countries," said Stalin. "We must catch up in ten years, or we shall be crushed." In 1928, he announced the first Five Year Plan. It set gigantic targets for every kind of heavy industry.

The people responded to Stalin's call. They set to work with energy and enthusiasm. Across the Soviet Union, armies of volunteer workers lived in tents, sharing beds in shifts, as they built vast new coal, iron and steel works, massive factories and Europe's largest dam on the River Dnieper.

AGRICULTURE

Stalin tightened his grip over the peasants. He wanted them to increase production by giving up their own farms and working under communist orders on vast collective farms, called *kolkhoz*.

When the peasants resisted, their villages were surrounded by machine gunners. In a great wave of anger, millions of Russian peasants burned their crops and slaughtered their cows and pigs, rather than hand them over to the new collective farms.

STALIN'S PRISON CAMPS

Stalin built up a vast system of prison camps, called Gulags. They became a vital part of the Soviet economy. During Stalin's rule, on average eight million prisoners slaved in the Gulags' deadly conditions, opening up frozen and remote areas of the country.

KEY

- Prison camps
- Tundra (frozen land)
- Dense forest
- Areas set aside for prison camps alone
- Railways built by prisoners
- Canal built by prisoners

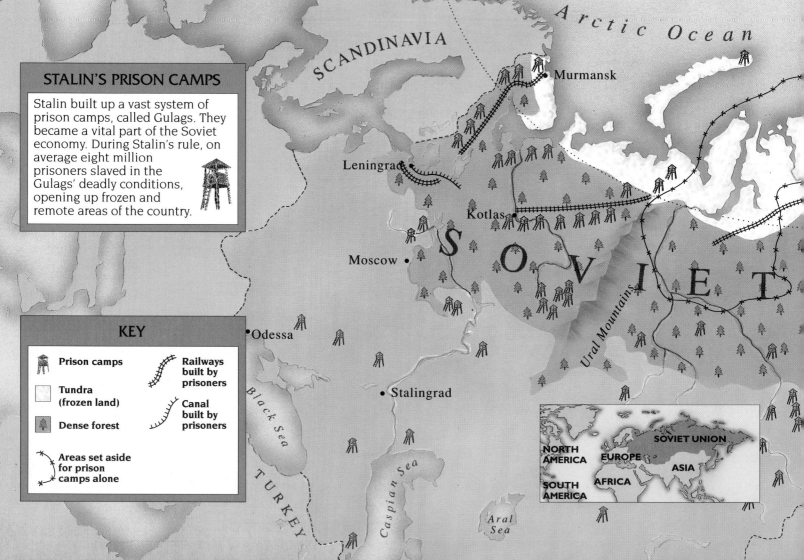

Map labels: SCANDINAVIA, Arctic Ocean, Murmansk, Leningrad, Kotlas, Moscow, Odessa, Stalingrad, Black Sea, TURKEY, Caspian Sea, Aral Sea, Ural Mountains, SOVIET

NORTH AMERICA, SOUTH AMERICA, EUROPE, AFRICA, ASIA, SOVIET UNION

CHAOS AND FAMINE

Millions of peasants were denounced as enemies of the people, and sent to prison camps in remote areas. In the chaos, few crops were sown. In 1932-33 up to three million people died in a man-made famine which swept through the Ukraine. People ate mice, ants or bark to survive. But factory workers received just enough food to keep up production.

These prisoners, who were known as *zeks*, are dragging a massive cable. Others mined gold, felled trees and laid railways.

THE GREAT TERROR

By 1934, Stalin was determined to get rid of anyone who opposed him. No one was safe. For little or no reason, millions of men and women were imprisoned, tortured or shot in the purges of the "Great Terror". Survivors were sent to join the peasants in the prison camps, where few lived longer than a couple of years.

A Gulag watchtower. Prisoners were kept cold and hungry, and were treated brutally.

THE AFTERMATH

By 1938 the Cheka, or State Police, had files on more than half the population of the cities. One in twenty of all the people in the Soviet Union had been arrested, and millions had died. The Terror had finally run its course. But now the Soviet people faced another deadly onslaught. In Germany, Adolf Hitler was preparing for war.

During World War Two, Hitler's forces were to invade the western part of the Soviet Union. Supplies from the industries in the Gulags helped the Soviet Union to survive Germany's attack.

NORYLLAG

It is said that several hundred camps of complete isolation were built within this region, in places impossible to escape from.

DALSTROI

UNION

Dalstroi region, over 1,000 miles (1,600km) long, was uninhabited except for prison camps.

Sea of Okhotsk

CHINA

FACT BOX

INDUSTRIALIZATION

Stalin saw electrification as the key to industrial progress. In 1928 the Soviet Union produced only 5,000 million units of electricity. By 1940 this had climbed almost tenfold to 48,300 million units. In the same period, steel production grew rapidly, to four times its previous level.

TARGETS

Failure to meet targets set by the Five Year Plans was a crime against the state. Factory directors became so desperate to reach their impossibly high targets that some ambushed freight trains to steal scarce raw materials they carried. This was less dangerous than failing to reach the targets.

STAKHANOVITES

Workers who surpassed their targets were hailed as heroes. They were known as *Stakhanovites*, after a Ukrainian miner, Alexei Stakhanov. It was said that he hewed 104 tonnes (tons) of coal in a shift instead of the usual seven. In fact his team gave him a lot of help.

The Stakhanovite movement created many heroes, from steel workers to milkmaids whose cows produced record levels of milk. They were treated as celebrities, to encourage others to follow their example. But many became unpopular with their workmates, who resented their success.

These women are learning to read and write. A massive literacy campaign, which reached millions of people in the first ten years of Soviet rule, was one of communism's great early achievements.

WORLD WAR TWO

In the 1930s, the German leader, Adolf Hitler, started to break the terms of the Versailles Treaty. He began by rearming Germany and by sending soldiers into the Rhineland on France's border. He also formed an alliance with Italy's leader, Benito Mussolini.

A British wartime identity card. Every citizen had one.

The war separated families. This baby girl was born in 1939. Her photo was taken to send to her father, on the frontline in 1940.

THE ANSCHLUSS

One of Hitler's aims was to gain control of countries where German-speakers lived. His first target was Austria, which was put under pressure to unite with Germany. Austria's Chancellor asked the people to take part in a referendum (vote) to decide if that was what they wanted. Before the vote took place, in March 1938 German troops entered Austria. This joining of Austria and Germany is called the Anschluss ("union"). It was forbidden by the Treaty of Versailles.

Here Austrians greet German soldiers. Many Austrians agreed with the Anschluss.

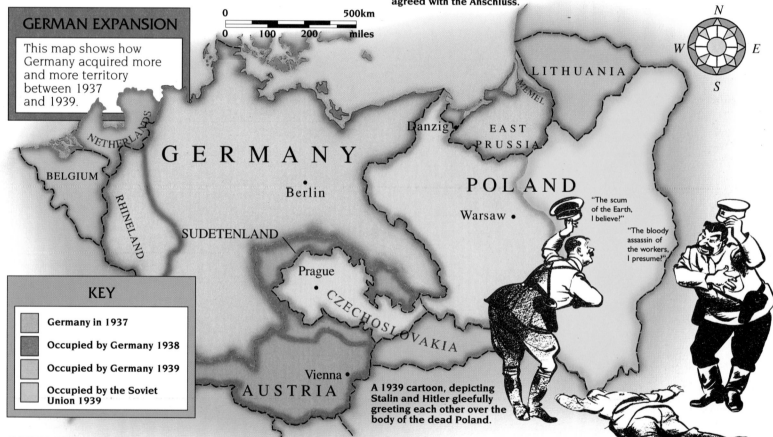

GERMAN EXPANSION

This map shows how Germany acquired more and more territory between 1937 and 1939.

0 — 500km
0   100   200   miles

LITHUANIA

MEMEL

Danzig

EAST PRUSSIA

GERMANY

Berlin

POLAND

Warsaw

RHINELAND

NETHERLANDS

BELGIUM

SUDETENLAND

Prague

CZECHOSLOVAKIA

Vienna

AUSTRIA

KEY

- Germany in 1937
- Occupied by Germany 1938
- Occupied by Germany 1939
- Occupied by the Soviet Union 1939

"The scum of the Earth, I believe?"

"The bloody assassin of the workers, I presume?"

A 1939 cartoon, depicting Stalin and Hitler gleefully greeting each other over the body of the dead Poland.

HITLER ADVANCES

France and Britain protested, but did nothing to stop the Anschluss. In September 1938, German troops occupied the Sudetenland in Czechoslovakia. The British Prime Minister tried to appease (pacify) Hitler, signing an agreement allowing him to keep the territory. Hitler now went in search of more *Lebensraum*, or "living space" for Germans.

British Prime Minister Chamberlain declares that his agreement with Hitler is "peace for our time".

ATTACK ON POLAND

Within six months, Germany occupied the rest of Czechoslovakia and also Memel in Lithuania. Stirred to action, Britain and France promised to help Poland, Romania and Greece if they were attacked. In August 1939, the Soviet Union and Germany signed a non-aggression pact. Secretly, they agreed to divide Poland up between them.

On September 1, Hitler invaded Poland. Britain and France had no choice but to declare war. The Poles fought bravely, but by the end of September the Germans had occupied the western half of their country, while the Soviets had occupied the east.

BLITZKRIEG

The first six months of the war were surprisingly uneventful. A small British Expeditionary Force crossed to France and all sides prepared for war. American journalists called it a "phony war". Then in April 1940, the Germans swept into neutral Denmark and Norway. They attacked Belgium, the Netherlands and Luxembourg, and pushed on into France. The Germans used the speed of tanks and planes in a tactic known as Blitzkrieg, or "lightning war".

As well as planes and tanks, German soldiers used motorcycles to speed their way across Europe.

The advance across Europe. German forces moved across Belgium, the Netherlands, Luxembourg and into France with frightening speed. They reached the English Channel within a week.

FACT BOX

THE AXIS POWERS

Germany's allies in the war were Italy, Romania, Bulgaria, Slovakia and Japan. Together they were known as the Axis Powers.

THE ALLIES

Those countries which fought against the Axis Powers and on the side of Britain and France were known as the Allies. They included Australia, New Zealand, South Africa, Canada and all other countries of the British Empire. The Soviet Union and the USA joined the Allies later in the war.

DUNKIRK

The Dunkirk Evacuation was code-named Operation Dynamo. A fleet of naval ships and civilian vessels ferried 338,000 soldiers back to Britain. The whole operation took nine days.

FALL OF PARIS

Paris fell to the German army on June 14, 1940. On June 25, a new French government led by Marshal Pétain, a World War One veteran, signed an armistice with Germany and Italy.

THE DUNKIRK EVACUATION

In May 1940, British and French troops were pushed back to a strip of land around Dunkirk. To save them from capture, a rescue operation was mounted. The Royal Navy, with the help of hundreds of private boats, ferried troops back to England. Northern France was occupied by Germany and the south, known as Vichy-France, was ruled by a German-controlled government at Vichy.

This 1939 Christmas card was printed for soldiers of the British Expeditionary Force to send back to their families.

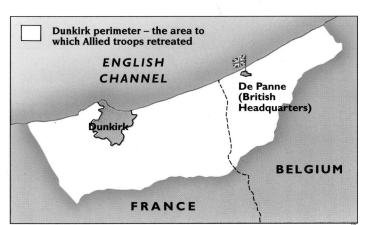

Dunkirk perimeter – the area to which Allied troops retreated

The area around Dunkirk, from which the British Expeditionary Force and some French troops were evacuated.

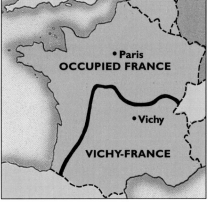

Occupied France and Vichy-France.

German Messerschmidt 109E

A British Vickers Supermarine Spitfire, flown in the Battle of Britain. It was one of the most successful fighters in the war.

THE BATTLE OF BRITAIN

With the support of the British Empire, Britain kept fighting. To subdue her, Hitler planned to invade. But to do this he realized that first he would have to wipe out the Royal Air Force. In August and September 1940, the Battle of Britain raged in the skies. Despite heavy losses, the RAF kept the German airforce, the Luftwaffe, at bay.

The Luftwaffe then changed tactics. It began to bomb British cities at night to crush morale. Bombers raided night after night, from September 1940 to May 1941 in a prolonged attack known as the Blitz. British bombers, in turn, pounded German cities. Civilians were now in the frontline. Many were killed or lost their homes and possessions.

There were eight machine guns in the wings.

THE WAR SPREADS

A British child's food rationing book. Ration books were issued to all.

By the end of 1940, much of Europe was under German occupation. Italy had also entered the war on Germany's side. Together they were known as the Axis Powers. With much of Europe occupied, Britain and its allies were now alone in resisting the Nazi threat.

Erwin Rommel, who commanded the Axis forces in North Africa.

BATTLE OF THE ATLANTIC

In order to continue the war, Britain relied on supply by ship. Battles took place at sea and German aircraft and U-boats (submarines), sank many supply ships. This was a serious threat to the Allies. In response, ships sailed in groups, called convoys, protected by warships. They also used a new tracking device called sonar to find and destroy the U-boats. This struggle, called the Battle of the Atlantic, continued to the end of the war.

HELP FROM THE USA

Although the USA did not enter the war straight away, President Roosevelt persuaded his government to support the Allies against Nazi Germany. Help was given through the Lend-Lease Act of 1941. The act enabled the USA to send supplies to any country if this action might help defend the USA itself. This meant that essential supplies of food, arms and materials could be sent to Britain to help them in the war effort.

The men, women and children left at home in Britain also threw themselves into the war effort. Food and clothes were rationed and everyone made an effort to save materials. A famous slogan, "Dig for Victory", encouraged people to grow their own food.

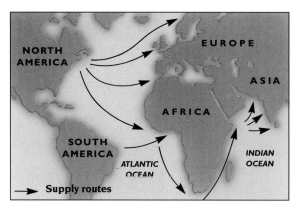

Allied supply routes across the oceans. To try to foil German attacks in the Atlantic, merchant ships sailed in convoys, guarded by warships.

British women working on a farm during the war. Known as the "Land Army", they took the place of male farmworkers who were away fighting. Women also did other jobs, such as working in arms factories and on buses and trains.

WAR IN NORTH AFRICA

From its colonies of Libya and Ethiopia, Italy attacked the Allies in North Africa. Successful at first, they were soon pushed back. To support them, Hitler sent in his Afrika Korps troops under Field Marshall Rommel. In 1941, the Germans advanced and by mid-1942, Rommel was just 100km (60 miles) away from Egypt – the British stronghold in North Africa. After losing a fierce battle at El Alamein, the Axis forces retreated, finally evacuating to Sicily.

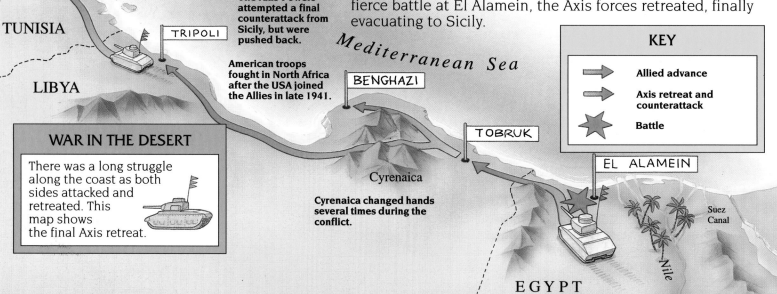

The Axis Powers attempted a final counterattack from Sicily, but were pushed back.

American troops fought in North Africa after the USA joined the Allies in late 1941.

WAR IN THE DESERT

There was a long struggle along the coast as both sides attacked and retreated. This map shows the final Axis retreat.

Cyrenaica changed hands several times during the conflict.

KEY

→ Allied advance

→ Axis retreat and counterattack

★ Battle

WAR AGAINST THE SOVIETS

In June 1941, Hitler went back on his pact with Stalin and ordered the invasion of the Soviet Union. Forgetting past tensions, the Soviets entered into an alliance with Britain. The Germans had expected the campaign to last only a few weeks, but fanatical Soviet resistance and the sheer size of the Soviet army held them back. The Russian winter arrived, and the Germans lacked equipment and suffered in the bitter cold. Far from victory, they were now fighting on two fronts.

German forces blasted their way into the Soviet Union. The invasion was codenamed Operation Barbarossa.

PEARL HARBOR

The Japanese, who were at war with China, had made a pact with Nazi Germany in 1936. With Europe at war, Japan saw an opportunity to expand into mainland Asia and also across the Pacific. Only the American Pacific fleet stood in their way. Without warning, on December 7, 1941, Japan invaded Malaya and Thailand and attacked the American fleet in Pearl Harbor, Hawaii, killing nearly 2,500 people. The USA immediately declared war on Japan, bringing both nations into World War Two.

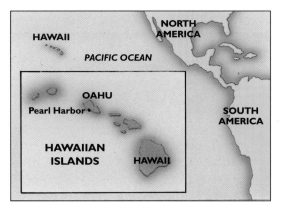

Pearl Harbor. 19 warships were sank or damaged, but the US aircraft carriers escaped – they were not there.

IN THE FAR EAST

At first the British forces were unable to stop the Japanese advance. Thousands of prisoners were taken by the Japanese and treated with such terrible cruelty that many died. The Japanese also conquered much territory in the Pacific, but their advance was finally halted in 1942. The British advanced overland and the Battles of the Coral Sea, Philippine Sea and Midway were victories for the US navy, although casualties were heavy. The Americans began to capture territory in the Pacific, island by island.

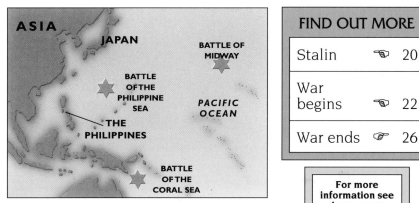

Major naval battles of the Pacific war. The Battle of the Philippine Sea was a particularly harsh defeat for Japan.

For more information see above pages.

THE FINAL SOLUTION

In 1941, the German leadership devised the "Final Solution" – all Jews were to be rounded up, sent to concentration camps and exterminated. The camps were heavily guarded and it was impossible to escape. While the war went on, Jews and other enemies of the Nazis suffered terribly as the Final Solution was carried out unmercifully.

Persecution of Jews had been going on for many years. Jews in German-occupied territory had to wear the yellow Star of David to identify them.

THE TURNING TIDE

In November 1942, General Montgomery defeated the Axis Powers in Egypt at the Battle of El Alamein. General Eisenhower led an Anglo-American landing in Morocco and Algeria, joined by the Vichy-French forces there. German forces were trapped in Tunisia and surrendered in May 1943. The German attack on the Soviet Union had failed and the U-boats were being driven out of the Atlantic. The Axis Powers were now halted and under pressure from all sides.

Anne Frank, a victim of the Nazis, whose diary became world famous. The writing says, "This is a photo of me as I wish I looked all the time. Then I might still have a chance of getting to Hollywood."

VICTORY FOR THE ALLIES

General de Gaulle, leader of the Free French army, inspects troops.

By July 1943, the Allies were in a stronger position than they had ever been. Allied troops gathered in Britain and North Africa, preparing for an invasion of mainland Europe. The liberation of Nazi-occupied territory was about to begin.

The route of the invasion of Italy, in which nearly half a million Allied troops took part.

ITALY INVADED

After their victory in North Africa, Allied troops landed in Italy on the Sicilian beaches. At first the Germans resisted, but were pushed back to the mainland. Welcomed by the people, the invading forces followed the retreating Germans north.

The Italian people were unhappy with their continued involvement in the war. Mussolini was ousted and imprisoned. The new Italian government made peace with the Allies and joined in against the Nazis. But the Allied campaign was hard-going and the push through Italy was slow.

A landing craft – a troop carrying ship used in the invasion of the Italian mainland and other seaborne invasions.

D-DAY

As the Allied troops were battling through Italy, Allied commanders were planning to launch an invasion of northern France. Troops and arms were collected together in southern England, waiting for the word to attack. The first day of the great invasion was to be codenamed "D-Day".

On June 6, 1944, landing craft in the English Channel made their way to the Normandy coast. Five strips of beaches had been identified as landing places for American, Canadian and British troops. Soldiers now poured ashore under German fire. Bombing raids had destroyed many German lines of communication, but heavy fighting still followed. The Allies did not break away from the Normandy coast until the end of July 1944.

FRANCE IS LIBERATED

The Allies began to fight their way through France, despite strong counterattacks. A second Allied army, containing units of General de Gaulle's Free French army, landed in southern France. On August 25, 1944, Paris itself was liberated due to the joint efforts of the Allies and the French Resistance – civilians who worked to undermine their German occupiers. Although it was not necessary to do this for military reasons, the Allies decided to enter Paris to boost the Allies' morale.

The next day de Gaulle led a triumphant march through the streets cheered by jubilant crowds. Belgium and the Netherlands were also liberated from German occupation. But German counterattacks still threatened the Allies' progress across Europe.

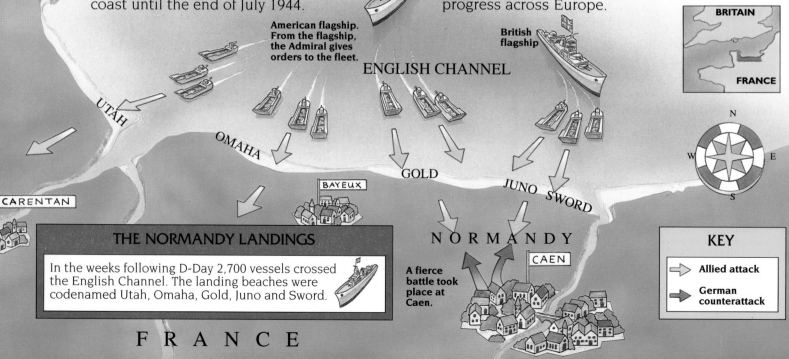

American flagship. From the flagship, the Admiral gives orders to the fleet.

British flagship

ENGLISH CHANNEL

THE NORMANDY LANDINGS

In the weeks following D-Day 2,700 vessels crossed the English Channel. The landing beaches were codenamed Utah, Omaha, Gold, Juno and Sword.

A fierce battle took place at Caen.

KEY

⇨ Allied attack

⇨ German counterattack

FRANCE

INTO GERMANY

In September 1944, Allied troops were crossing the western German frontier, but a struggle lay ahead of them. At Arnhem in the Netherlands, British paratroops tried to secure a bridge over the Rhine and were defeated with heavy losses, but this was only a temporary setback. Meanwhile, Soviet troops were advancing from the east.

HITLER'S LAST WEAPON

Hitler refused to acknowledge this dire situation. In June 1944, he ordered his new secret weapon to be put into action. This was the rocket-propelled flying bomb, called the V-1 ("V" stood for *Vergeltung*, meaning "Revenge"). Known as "doodlebugs", they were capable of reaching London from France.

Shortly after the V-1, an even greater threat was developed – the V-2. But Hitler's flying bombs could not save him. By spring 1945 the Allies were advancing from both sides. Unable to face defeat, Hitler killed himself on April 30. On May 8, the German government surrendered.

DEATH CAMPS DISCOVERED

As Allied armies moved across Europe, they made a terrible discovery. In the some of the areas they liberated were concentration camps where Jews, Slavs, gypsies, the mentally ill and enemies of the Nazis had been sent to work as slaves or simply to be exterminated under the Nazi's Final Solution.

The Allies liberated the surviving prisoners in the death camps, but it was too late for most of them. Most had died of disease or overwork, or had been murdered. About 15 million people in all were killed in this way. Six million of these people were Jews. This event is known as the Holocaust.

JAPAN SURRENDERS

Meanwhile, the Allies were still fighting Japan. American troops were advancing in the Pacific, Allied armies were moving into Burma, and the Soviets invaded Manchuria. Japan was already being heavily bombed, when a devastating weapon was used against it. On August 6, 1945 the US Air Force dropped an atom bomb on Hiroshima. Two days later a second bomb was dropped on Nagasaki. Both cities were completely destroyed and Japan surrendered on August 14, 1945.

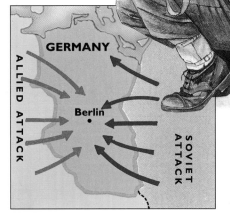

A British paratrooper. Over 20,000 Allied troops were dropped into the Netherlands. 8,000 British paratroopers landed at Arnhem, of which only 2,000 escaped.

In April 1945, the Allies were closing in on Berlin from both east and west.

Europe's concentration camps. Those in Poland were set up specifically as extermination camps.

Japanese territory in mid-1943. US marines advanced across it.

Japanese territory in August 1945. Japan itself was not invaded.

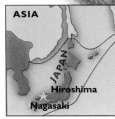

Hiroshima and Nagasaki – the cities destroyed by atomic bombs.

The "mushroom cloud" explosion of an atomic bomb.

FACT BOX

FRENCH RESISTANCE

In occupied France, some anti-Nazis took up arms and worked under cover to help the Allies. Known as the French Resistance, or the Maquis, they sabotaged German equipment and helped Allied prisoners to escape back to Britain. Resistance groups flourished in all occupied countries.

THE JULY PLOT

Hitler had always had enemies, but by mid-1944, they were becoming bold. In July, senior members of his staff attempted to kill him with a bomb, in the so-called July Plot. They failed and the leaders were executed. Some opted for suicide.

WINSTON CHURCHILL

Churchill was one of the great Allied leaders of the war. He had served in the army before becoming a war correspondent during the Boer War. He became Prime Minister of Britain in May 1940. His stirring speeches helped to keep morale high and keep the Allies together.

MUSSOLINI'S FATE

A daring German raid rescued Mussolini from his prison in the Apennine Mountains. His rescuers flew him to northern Italy where he was set up as leader of a puppet Italian government by Hitler. In April 1945, as the war drew to a close, Mussolini was captured by Italian partisans and executed.

HIROSHIMA

Hiroshima was flattened by the atomic bomb. An 8km (5 mile) high cloud covered the city and the explosion was said to be as bright as the sun. 80,000 were killed and within a year 60,000 more died of injuries and disease caused by the bomb's radiation.

EUROPE DIVIDES

By the end of World War Two, much of Europe was in ruins. While the people started to rebuild their lives, their leaders set about making a lasting peace. But without a common enemy to unite them, the bonds between the Allies were soon to unravel.

British Prime Minister Churchill, US President Roosevelt and Stalin, the Soviet leader, at Yalta.

THE AFTERMATH

The war created millions of orphans and widows. Throughout Europe, air raids and street fighting had turned cities into rubble. Homes, factories and farms were devastated. Shelter and food were in desperately short supply. Many went hungry.

Millions had been forced away from their homelands by the war. Great trudging masses of people were trying to get back home, or to build a new life elsewhere. Refugees, ex-slave workers, freed prisoners of war, and survivors of the concentration camps – all were on the move. As the new borders were drawn in areas such as Poland and the Baltic coast, people who for generations had been settled were now forced to uproot and return to their original homelands. Many fled west because they did not want to live under a communist regime.

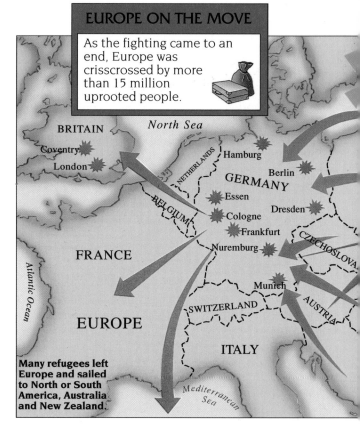

EUROPE ON THE MOVE

As the fighting came to an end, Europe was crisscrossed by more than 15 million uprooted people.

Many refugees left Europe and sailed to North or South America, Australia and New Zealand.

BRITAIN · North Sea · Coventry · London · NETHERLANDS · Hamburg · Berlin · GERMANY · BELGIUM · Essen · Dresden · Cologne · FRANCE · Frankfurt · CZECHOSLOVA... · Nuremburg · Atlantic Ocean · Munich · SWITZERLAND · AUSTRIA · EUROPE · ITALY · Mediterranean Sea

UNITED NATIONS

The old League of Nations, set up after World War One, had failed to prevent another global war. In 1945, world leaders decided to set up a new organization. The United Nations (or UN), as it was called, had more power than the old League of Nations because now both the superpowers, the USA and Soviet Union, were members. The UN set out its aim: "to save succeeding generations from the scourge of war".

The symbol of the United Nations. The olive branches represent peace.

Much of Europe was bombed to ruins. Here in Dresden and elsewhere, the *Trümmerfrauen*, "women of the rubble", rebuilt their cities brick by brick.

GERMANY'S FUTURE

In February 1945, now certain of victory, the Allied leaders had held a conference at Yalta by the Black Sea to discuss Germany's future. The Soviet Union, which had lost 20 million people, wanted to punish Germany for the war. But the other leaders wanted to avoid the problems that had brought Hitler to power. Germany (and her capital city, Berlin) was to be divided and occupied by foreign powers. She was forbidden to make weapons or to have an army capable of military action.

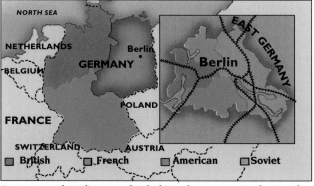

NORTH SEA · NETHERLANDS · Berlin · GERMANY · BELGIUM · FRANCE · POLAND · SWITZERLAND · AUSTRIA · EAST GERMANY · Berlin

☐ British   ☐ French   ☐ American   ☐ Soviet

Germany and Berlin were divided into four zones. Berlin, inside the Soviet zone, had special access routes to the West.

GROWING SUSPICIONS

As the war drew to a close, the superpowers grew suspicions of each other. Stalin was alarmed to discover that the USA had built the atom bomb – and furious that it had dropped two of them on Japan without consulting him. The Soviets urgently started work on their own bomb. For their part, American leaders suspected that the Soviet Union wanted to build a communist empire across Europe and beyond.

Thousands of anti-communist Russians were forced back to the Soviet Union against their will. Many were executed or sent to prison camps in Siberia.

KEY

→ 1 million concentration camp survivors and refugees

→ 5 million Russians

→ 11 million Germans

→ Russians leaving for the Baltic States

→ Baltic peoples

→ Poles

✸ Some bombed cities

US TROOPS AND AID

America watched with alarm as Eastern European nations fell under Soviet influence. Would Western Europe, hungry and demoralized after the war, turn to communism? In 1947, both Greece and Turkey teetered on the brink of communist revolution. US President Truman sent American aid and weapons to support the "free peoples" there against what he saw as a communist threat.

The US offered European governments massive amounts of aid, in the form of food, goods and cash to rebuild factories, roads and transportation. Eagerly, the nations of Western Europe accepted. But the Soviet Union and other communist countries refused the offer. The Marshall Plan, as it was called, pumped $14,000,000,000 into Western Europe between 1948-52. As a result, the West recovered quickly from the war.

This poster promoted the new Common Market, set up in 1955 to strengthen trade in Western Europe. It later became known as the European Community. The region's industry flourished with Marshall Plan money received from the US.

FACT BOX

NUREMBERG TRIALS

In 1945-47 at Nuremberg in Germany, 177 Germans and Austrians were tried for war crimes. Survivors of the concentration camps gave harrowing evidence against them. In total, 25 Nazi leaders were sentenced to death for crimes against humanity, and 117 were sent to prison.

KATYN FOREST MASSACRE

Tensions arose at the Nuremberg Trials over the mass graves discovered in Katyn Forest in Poland. Thousands of Polish officers had been massacred there in 1940. Soviet and Nazi generals accused each other's troops. To this day, neither side has admitted that they carried out the mass killings.

EASTERN EUROPE

In 1945, Soviet troops raced across Eastern Europe, freeing it from Nazi control. They stayed on to create a communist zone right along the Soviet border. Despite agreeing at Yalta to a "free and independent Poland", Stalin now insisted on communist leaders there. He had the old rulers of Bulgaria and Romania arrested as Nazi sympathizers, and replaced them with his own supporters. Even Czechoslovakia, with its stronger democratic traditions, soon fell to Stalin's pressure.

Europe divides. In 1946, Churchill spoke of an "iron curtain" separating the communist East from the capitalist West.

BERLIN AIRLIFT

Berlin, where East and West were face to face, became a focus for tension. In 1948, frustrated by this island of capitalism inside communist territory, Stalin blockaded all road and rail routes into West Berlin.

Planes brought basic rations into West Berlin – including food for the city's zoo animals.

Defiantly, the Western powers started a massive, regular airlift of food, fuel and mail. The Soviets knew that to shoot down the planes would lead to war. For nearly a year, West Berliners survived on airlifted rations. Eventually, in 1949, the Soviet Union backed down. East and West Germany became two countries.

THE BIRTH OF ISRAEL

Jewish children who came from Yemen to settle in the new state of Israel.

The Jewish people had been stateless since the Romans forced them out of Palestine in AD98. Since the end of the nineteenth century, Jews had campaigned for a nation. As news of the Holocaust emerged after World War Two, support grew for the idea. Palestine, the Jews' ancient homeland, seemed the obvious place.

Many Arabs fled from Palestine in 1948. They hoped to return later.

ZIONISM

Zionism is the belief that Jewish people should have their own independent homeland. The Zionist movement, founded in the late nineteenth century, flourished among European Jews in a climate of widespread anti-Semitism (hatred of Jewish people). Some rulers encouraged violent attacks against Jews, as a distraction from other problems. Zionists dreamed of a mass return to the Jewish homeland, Palestine.

BRITISH PROMISES

During World War One, the British promised to press for a Jewish state in Palestine. They hoped to win Jewish support in the United States, which had just entered the war. But the British had also promised an independent state to the Arabs who lived in Palestine, who were mainly Muslims. They did this to undermine their Turkish rulers, who were Germany's allies in the war. After the war, Britain was given a mandate to rule Palestine when the Ottoman Empire was broken up.

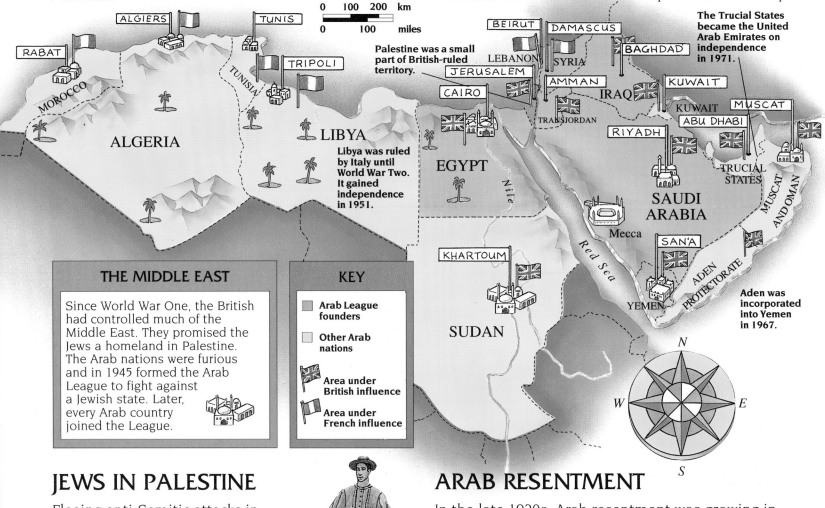

0 100 200 km
0 100 miles

Palestine was a small part of British-ruled territory.

The Trucial States became the United Arab Emirates on independence in 1971.

Libya was ruled by Italy until World War Two. It gained independence in 1951.

Aden was incorporated into Yemen in 1967.

THE MIDDLE EAST

Since World War One, the British had controlled much of the Middle East. They promised the Jews a homeland in Palestine. The Arab nations were furious and in 1945 formed the Arab League to fight against a Jewish state. Later, every Arab country joined the League.

KEY

- ■ Arab League founders
- ☐ Other Arab nations
- ⚑ Area under British influence
- ⚑ Area under French influence

JEWS IN PALESTINE

Fleeing anti-Semitic attacks in Europe, Jews had been settling in Palestine since the turn of the century. They bought land from Arab landlords. The settlers endured harsh conditions at first. Much of their land was stony or marshy. Many died of malaria. But full of hope, energy and idealism, they built new cities and set up communal farms, called *kibbutzim*.

An early Jewish settler working on the land in Palestine.

ARAB RESENTMENT

In the late 1920s, Arab resentment was growing in Palestine. In 1929 thousands of Arabs rioted in protest at Jewish immigration. Unrest spread quickly. To protect themselves, Jewish settlers later formed an armed security force called the Hagannah.

The British, now responsible for ruling Palestine, were getting desperate. To try to calm the Arabs, after 1933 they limited the number of Jews allowed to enter and settle in Palestine each month to just 1,500. They ignored the growing threat to European Jews from Nazi Germany.

JEWS FLEE HITLER

In 1933 the Nazis, fanatical anti-Semites, took power in Germany. Thousands of Jews fled for Palestine. But the British turned most away. Many drowned, and some were even returned to Europe where they were rounded up by the Nazis.

A refugee ship bound for Palestine. Even after World War Two, the British still turned away most Jewish refugees and survivors of the Nazi death camps.

FACT BOX

THE MUFTI OF JERUSALEM

In 1921, the British appointed a vicious anti-Semite, Mohammed Amin al-Husseini, as senior judge, or *Mufti*, of Jerusalem. He organized the murder of many moderate Arabs who were prepared to live side by side with Jewish settlers.

HEBREW, THE NATIONAL LANGUAGE

Hebrew had always been the Jews' language of prayer. It was not used for everyday talk or writing. But early settlers in Palestine decided to use Hebrew, as part of their national identity. As Jewish immigrants arrived from all over the world, they learned Hebrew, a single language which bound them all together.

"OPERATION MAGIC CARPET"

Large Jewish communities in Arab countries had been allowed to live more or less peacefully until Israel was formed. But hostility to the new state meant that Jews in Arab countries became the target of attacks. Many came to settle in Israel. In "Operation Magic Carpet", between 1949-50, 49,000 Jews were airlifted from Yemen to safety in Israel.

TERRORISM

After World War Two, terrorism escalated in Palestine. Jerusalem was besieged by Arab guerilla fighters. Jewish terrorists killed 250 people at the Arab village of Deir Yassin. Although this was condemned by the Zionist leadership, the Arabs struck back, ambushing a medical convoy, killing many doctors and nurses. A world exhausted by war wanted a simple solution to the problems in Palestine. The United Nations suggested dividing the area into two halves, one Jewish and one Arab.

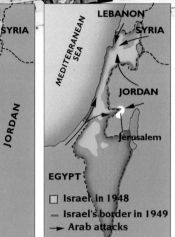

Palestine in 1947, as the UN planned to divide it. Jews and Arabs were to have an equal share.

Israel in 1949. At first, Arab attacks forced Israeli troops back, but in the end Israel won some extra land.

A NEW STATE

The state of Israel was declared on 14 May 1948. The very next day the armies of five Arab nations attacked Israel. In Israel's War of Independence, as it became known, Arab troops outnumbered Israeli forces three to one. But united and fighting for survival, the Israelis won. They took some land which the UN had allocated to the Arabs. The rest became part of the new kingdom of Jordan.

The Zionists' dream had come true. The new state of Israel started to build schools, universities, hospitals and industries. But the war had brought a cease-fire without peace. Arab leaders called for the destruction of the Zionist state.

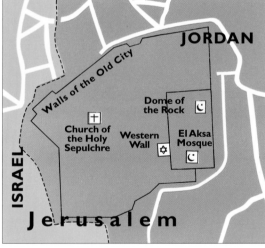

Part of the city of Jerusalem. Sacred to Jews, Muslims and Christians, in 1948 Jerusalem was divided after Israel's war of independence. Jews could not go to pray at holy sites in Arab territory, such as the Western Wall.

THE PALESTINIANS

Around 300,000 Arabs had fled from Palestine on the eve of war. Now homeless and stateless, they became known as the Palestinians. Many lived in refugee camps in the countries on Israel's borders. During the 1950s and 60s, they believed that the Arab states would help them to return to Israel. But despite strong words, Arab leaders did little. Instead, they used the plight of the Palestinians to keep up hatred of Israel. Around 200,000 Arabs remained in Israel in 1948. They had the right to vote, but were second class citizens, with poorer education, health care and housing than Jewish citizens.

A Palestinian refugee camp in Jordan. At first, many camps had no running water or electricity.

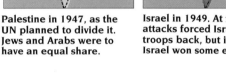

INDEPENDENCE FOR ASIA

As the century progressed, demands for independence from European colonial powers grew steadily in Asia. Some nations achieved this peacefully, but for others it was a violent and bitter struggle.

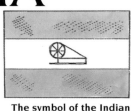

The symbol of the Indian National Congress Party.

THE INDIAN NATIONAL CONGRESS

In 1885, the Indian National Congress Party was founded by a group of middle-class Indians. They wanted a share in government, but Britain was reluctant to relax its control over its prize colony. The Indian Acts of 1909, 1919 and 1935 gave Indians a say in government, but not as much as they wanted.

In 1915, a young lawyer called Mohandas Karamchand Gandhi joined the Indian National Congress. He had already campaigned for Indian rights in South Africa (where many Indians lived). Gradually he emerged as the leader, encouraging non-violent protest, such as marches. He was imprisoned several times, but went on hunger strike to continue his protest.

Gandhi was assassinated by a Hindu fanatic in 1948. He became known to the Hindu people as the *Mahatma* **or "Great Soul".**

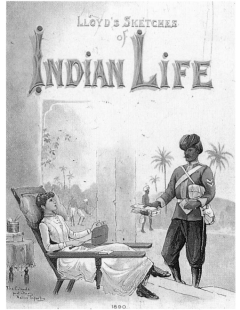

This illustration of 1890 shows the luxurious life of the British in India.

INDIA AND PAKISTAN

In India there were two main religious groups – Hindus and Muslims. The Indian National Congress was supported by Hindus, while the Muslims had their own party called the Muslim League. At first, the two parties worked together for independence, but Muslims were worried that they would have less say in an independent India. The Muslim League insisted on a separate state. Gandhi agreed, although he had hoped to keep India together.

After World War Two, Britain was struggling to rebuild itself and had to let its colonies go. In 1947, the Indian Empire became independent and two states were created – India for Hindus and Pakistan for Muslims.

Muslims from Hindu areas migrating to Pakistan. Thousands of refugees left their homes amid much violence.

NEW BEGINNINGS

Other parts of Asia had also been colonized in the nineteenth century. In World War Two, Japan had attacked the colonies, including Malaya (now Malaysia), Dutch East Indies (Indonesia), Burma (Myanmar) and the Philippines. It also occupied parts of Vietnam, where the Japanese became targets for Vietnamese nationalists, led by Ho Chi Minh. Calls for independence in Asia gathered strength, especially after Japan's defeat. The people no longer wanted to be dominated by foreign powers.

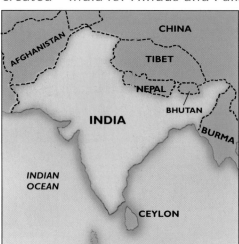

The Indian sub-continent in 1945. It had been ruled by Britain since the eighteenth century.

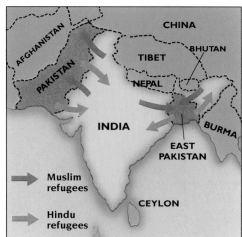

The separate states of India and Pakistan in 1947. East Pakistan became Bangladesh in 1971.

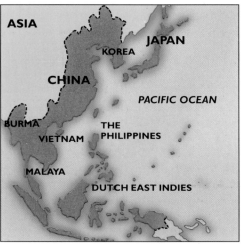

Japanese territory during World War Two. The Japanese wanted an empire in Asia.

FRENCH INDOCHINA

After World War Two, France tried to regain control over its colonies in French Indochina. Vietnamese nationalists were opposed to this and war broke out in 1946. French forces made a huge effort to win back their colony, but were no match for the Vietnamese guerillas in the jungles. The nationalists set up a republic in the north, which came under communist control.

After crushing the French at Dien Bien Phu, Vietnam declared itself independent in 1954. But it was a divided country – the communists still controlled the north, while the south was supported by the democratic powers in the West. Cambodia and Laos became independent in 1953.

Three independent countries emerged from the former French Indochina – Laos, Vietnam and Cambodia.

FACT BOX

DIEN BIEN PHU

This was the decisive battle in the war for independence in Vietnam. French airborne troops seized the village of Dien Bien Phu in November 1953 and a battle followed. The French were besieged and defeated in May 1954. Two months later, France signed an armistice and withdrew its troops from Vietnam.

THE DUTCH EMPIRE

After the British and the French, the Dutch empire was the third biggest. Most of it was in Indonesia (then called the Dutch East Indies).

Vietnamese villagers

The Thakin Party led the call for independence in Burma in the 1930s. Independence was granted in 1948. Renamed Myanmar, it is now under a military dictatorship.

A NEW ASIA

This map shows the modern borders of the Asian countries. It also shows which areas were colonized by which European powers. China was not colonized by any European nation, although at times European influence there was strong.

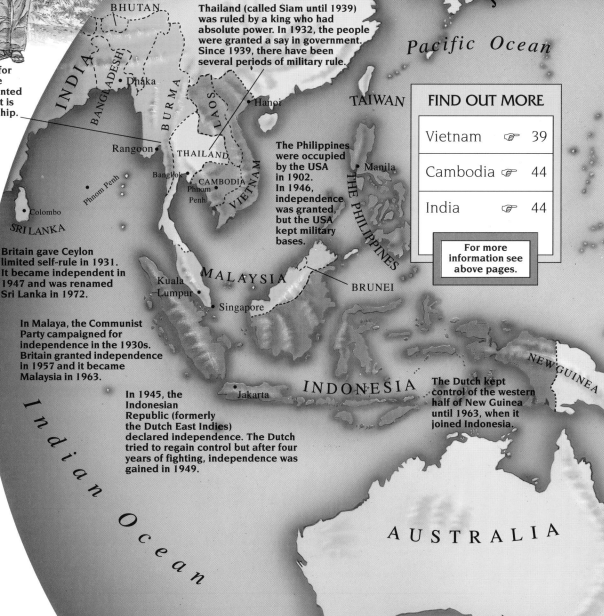

Thailand (called Siam until 1939) was ruled by a king who had absolute power. In 1932, the people were granted a say in government. Since 1939, there have been several periods of military rule.

The Philippines were occupied by the USA in 1902. In 1946, independence was granted, but the USA kept military bases.

Britain gave Ceylon limited self-rule in 1931. It became independent in 1947 and was renamed Sri Lanka in 1972.

In Malaya, the Communist Party campaigned for independence in the 1930s. Britain granted independence in 1957 and it became Malaysia in 1963.

In 1945, the Indonesian Republic (formerly the Dutch East Indies) declared independence. The Dutch tried to regain control but after four years of fighting, independence was gained in 1949.

The Dutch kept control of the western half of New Guinea until 1963, when it joined Indonesia.

FIND OUT MORE

Vietnam	☞	39
Cambodia	☞	44
India	☞	44

For more information see above pages.

KEY

Former colonies

- ■ USA
- ■ Dutch
- ■ French
- ■ British

This poster commemorates all the colonies that sent soldiers to fight on behalf of the Allies in World War Two.

A NEW AFRICA

After World War Two, African colonies, like their fellow colonies in Asia, began to demand independence. Europe was devastated by the war and could not hold onto its possessions abroad.

Stamps celebrating the independence of Ghana, Gambia, Congo and Nigeria.

ALGERIA

The French colony of Algeria was promised that after the war it would be given a share in its own government. France, though, did not keep her promise on this. In 1952, oil was discovered in Algeria and French settlers grew even more determined to stay, hoping that the oil might bring wealth. In 1954, war broke out. After eight years of bitter guerilla fighting, France finally granted Algeria her independence in 1962.

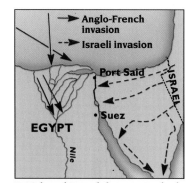

Algeria's oil fields. Pipelines take the oil from the desert to the coast for export.

An Algerian soldier. In the war of independence, women were required to fight.

EGYPT

In 1922, after nationalist protests, the British recognized Egypt as a constitutional monarchy but retained some powers, including control over Sudan. The British were keen to maintain some power in Egypt because of the Suez Canal. The canal (built between 1854 and 1869) is a vital short cut between the Mediterranean Sea and the Indian Ocean.

THE SUEZ CRISIS

In 1952, Colonel Nasser came to power in Egypt. In 1956, he brought the Suez Canal under Egyptian control, threatening British and French interests. Later that year Israel invaded Egypt, which gave Britain and France the opportunity to send troops on a pretence of restoring order. In reality, they wanted to restore control over the canal. Fierce protests, led by the United Nations, forced them to withdraw.

APARTHEID

After World War Two, South Africa's politics were dominated by the white minority – descendants of British and Dutch settlers who had colonized the area in past centuries.

In 1948, the National Party was in power. It introduced an official policy of apartheid, or "separateness". This meant that the different races, Asians, Africans and Europeans, were given different rights. In practice, whites were given more privileges and nonwhites had very little opportunity to improve their standard of living. Mixed marriages were forbidden and at first nonwhites were not allowed to vote or even share the same buses as whites. Anti-apartheid riots at Sharpeville in 1960 led to the death of 67 people.

Apartheid was internationally condemned. Protests from the British Commonwealth led to South Africa leaving it in 1961.

RHODESIA BECOMES ZIMBABWE

In Southern Rhodesia, the white Rhodesia Front Party wanted independence from Britain, but refused Britain's demands for the party to share power with the black Africans. In 1965, Southern Rhodesia made its Unilateral Declaration of Independence (UDI) from Britain. The white government ruled until 1979 when it was finally made to accept black majority rule. The country took the name Zimbabwe in 1980.

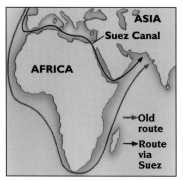

The canal is 162km (100 miles) long and 60m (197ft) wide. Before it was built, ships bound for Asia had to go around Africa.

British and French forces attacked Egyptian bases, and paratroops landed around Port Said, the entrance to the canal.

British colonies in Africa in 1945. Southern Rhodesia was renamed Rhodesia on UDI – its break from Britain.

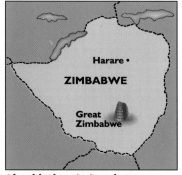

After black majority rule was brought in, Rhodesia was renamed Zimbabwe after the ancient stone ruins of Great Zimbabwe.

THE MAP OF AFRICA

Many borders of African countries are straight lines. This is because Africa was divided by its colonizers, without regard to traditional tribal borders. This has led to problems after independence, as many countries contain two or more peoples, with different languages and religions.

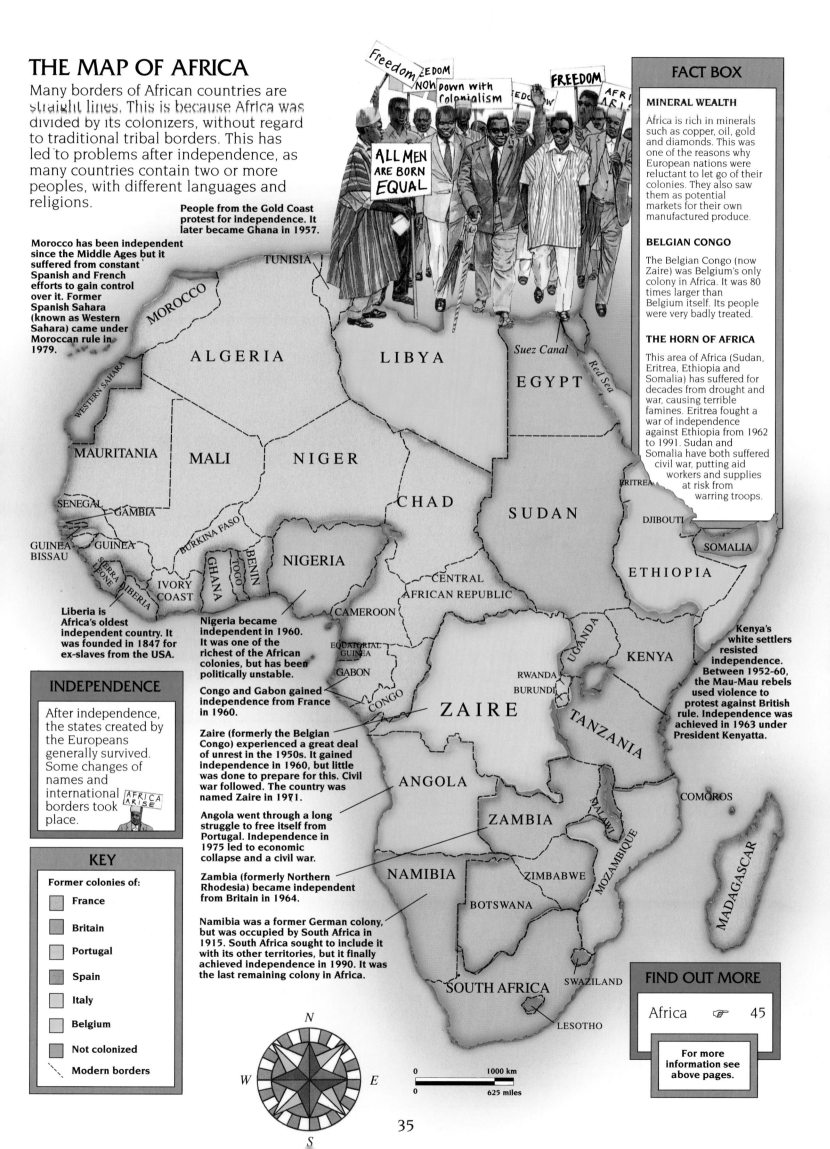

MINERAL WEALTH

Africa is rich in minerals such as copper, oil, gold and diamonds. This was one of the reasons why European nations were reluctant to let go of their colonies. They also saw them as potential markets for their own manufactured produce.

BELGIAN CONGO

The Belgian Congo (now Zaire) was Belgium's only colony in Africa. It was 80 times larger than Belgium itself. Its people were very badly treated.

THE HORN OF AFRICA

This area of Africa (Sudan, Eritrea, Ethiopia and Somalia) has suffered for decades from drought and war, causing terrible famines. Eritrea fought a war of independence against Ethiopia from 1962 to 1991. Sudan and Somalia have both suffered civil war, putting aid workers and supplies at risk from warring troops.

People from the Gold Coast protest for independence. It later became Ghana in 1957.

Morocco has been independent since the Middle Ages but it suffered from constant Spanish and French efforts to gain control over it. Former Spanish Sahara (known as Western Sahara) came under Moroccan rule in 1979.

ALL MEN ARE BORN EQUAL

Liberia is Africa's oldest independent country. It was founded in 1847 for ex-slaves from the USA.

Nigeria became independent in 1960. It was one of the richest of the African colonies, but has been politically unstable.

Congo and Gabon gained independence from France in 1960.

Zaire (formerly the Belgian Congo) experienced a great deal of unrest in the 1950s. It gained independence in 1960, but little was done to prepare for this. Civil war followed. The country was named Zaire in 1971.

Angola went through a long struggle to free itself from Portugal. Independence in 1975 led to economic collapse and a civil war.

Zambia (formerly Northern Rhodesia) became independent from Britain in 1964.

Namibia was a former German colony, but was occupied by South Africa in 1915. South Africa sought to include it with its other territories, but it finally achieved independence in 1990. It was the last remaining colony in Africa.

Kenya's white settlers resisted independence. Between 1952-60, the Mau-Mau rebels used violence to protest against British rule. Independence was achieved in 1963 under President Kenyatta.

INDEPENDENCE

After independence, the states created by the Europeans generally survived. Some changes of names and international borders took place.

AFRICA ARISE

KEY

Former colonies of:

- France
- Britain
- Portugal
- Spain
- Italy
- Belgium
- Not colonized
- – – Modern borders

Map labels

MOROCCO, TUNISIA, ALGERIA, LIBYA, EGYPT, Suez Canal, Red Sea, WESTERN SAHARA, MAURITANIA, MALI, NIGER, CHAD, SUDAN, ERITREA, DJIBOUTI, SENEGAL, GAMBIA, GUINEA BISSAU, GUINEA, BURKINA FASO, SIERRA LEONE, LIBERIA, IVORY COAST, GHANA, TOGO, BENIN, NIGERIA, CENTRAL AFRICAN REPUBLIC, SOMALIA, ETHIOPIA, CAMEROON, EQUATORIAL GUINEA, GABON, CONGO, ZAIRE, UGANDA, KENYA, RWANDA, BURUNDI, TANZANIA, ANGOLA, ZAMBIA, MALAWI, MOZAMBIQUE, COMOROS, NAMIBIA, ZIMBABWE, BOTSWANA, MADAGASCAR, SWAZILAND, LESOTHO, SOUTH AFRICA

N
W — E
S

| 0 | 1000 km |
| 0 | 625 miles |

Africa ☞ 45

For more information see above pages.

LATIN AMERICA

Latin America is the name given to Central and South America. Few of the countries in the region were involved in the two world wars, but they had plenty of conflicts of their own.

A South American shanty town – a slum area of make-do homes surrounding a city.

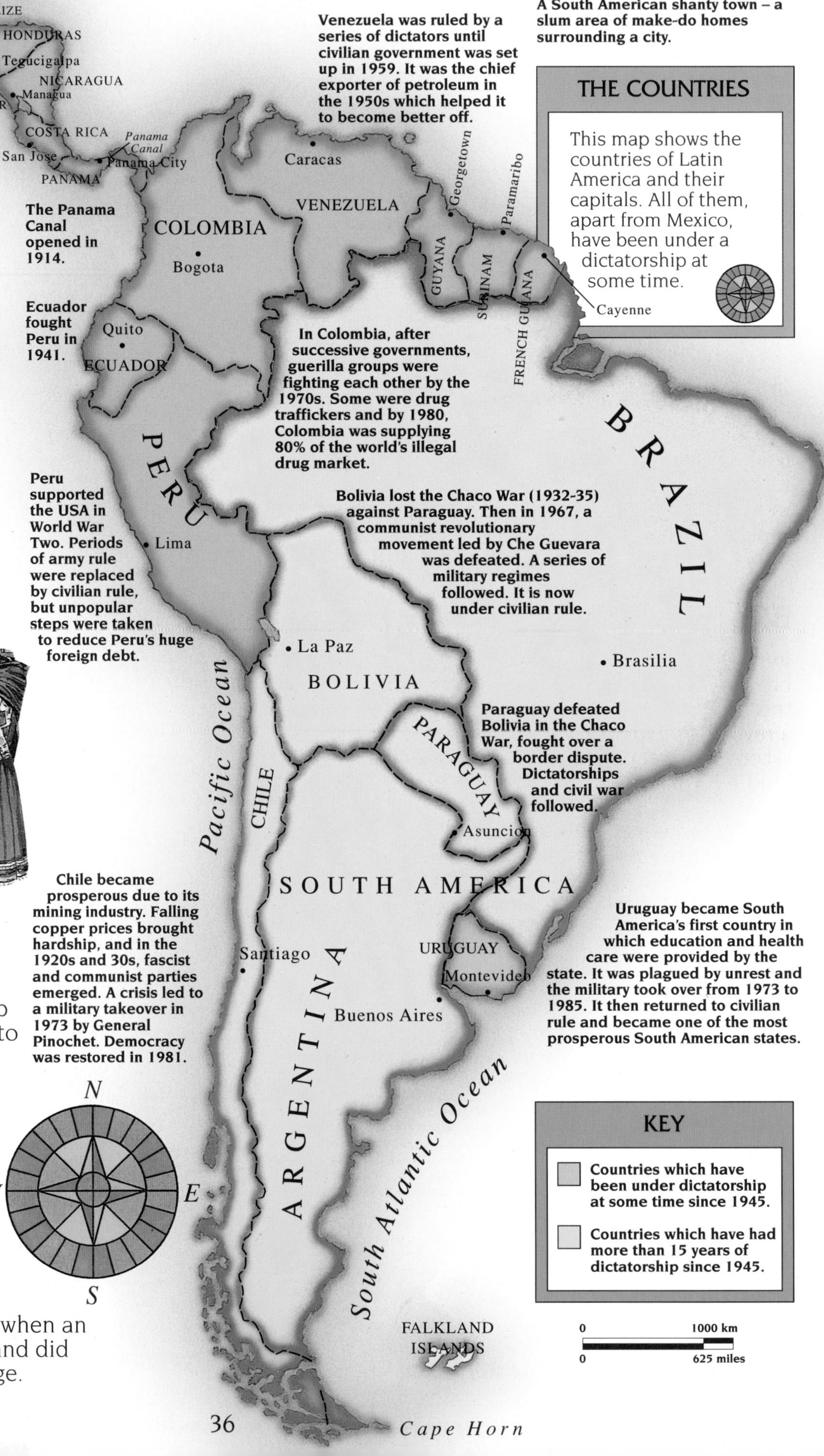

Mexico underwent a revolution in 1910-11 against the dictator Porfirio Diaz.

RICH AND POOR

Although many Latin American countries are rich in natural resources, such as agricultural land and minerals, many people are very poor. There are many conflicts in South America between different groups – landowners, the business community (which wants to develop natural resources), native South American Indians living in the forests and the poor living in city slums. Dictators grabbed power in many countries in order to bring stability, but this often led to abuses of power in which people were persecuted.

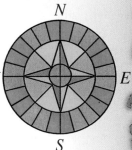

Peasant farmers from Peru. The population in South America has been steadily increasing in the twentieth century. As cities grew, peasants left their farms to find work, but most ended up desperately poor and living in slums.

FOREIGN DEBT

Many countries borrowed from world banks to help them develop industries. But they were unable to repay the money they borrowed. Mexico ran up one of the largest debts. Governments tried to boost the economy, but people were very poor. In the early 1980s Mexico, along with Argentina and Brazil, threatened to stop repaying the loans. Banks were thrown into a panic, but the situation was resolved by negotiation. In 1985, Mexico suffered even more when an earthquake killed 20,000 people and did billions of dollars worth of damage.

The Panama Canal opened in 1914.

Ecuador fought Peru in 1941.

GALAPAGOS ISLANDS

Peru supported the USA in World War Two. Periods of army rule were replaced by civilian rule, but unpopular steps were taken to reduce Peru's huge foreign debt.

Venezuela was ruled by a series of dictators until civilian government was set up in 1959. It was the chief exporter of petroleum in the 1950s which helped it to become better off.

In Colombia, after successive governments, guerilla groups were fighting each other by the 1970s. Some were drug traffickers and by 1980, Colombia was supplying 80% of the world's illegal drug market.

Bolivia lost the Chaco War (1932-35) against Paraguay. Then in 1967, a communist revolutionary movement led by Che Guevara was defeated. A series of military regimes followed. It is now under civilian rule.

Paraguay defeated Bolivia in the Chaco War, fought over a border dispute. Dictatorships and civil war followed.

Chile became prosperous due to its mining industry. Falling copper prices brought hardship, and in the 1920s and 30s, fascist and communist parties emerged. A crisis led to a military takeover in 1973 by General Pinochet. Democracy was restored in 1981.

Uruguay became South America's first country in which education and health care were provided by the state. It was plagued by unrest and the military took over from 1973 to 1985. It then returned to civilian rule and became one of the most prosperous South American states.

THE COUNTRIES

This map shows the countries of Latin America and their capitals. All of them, apart from Mexico, have been under a dictatorship at some time.

KEY

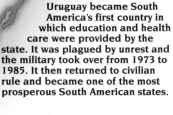

Countries which have been under dictatorship at some time since 1945.

Countries which have had more than 15 years of dictatorship since 1945.

| 0 | 1000 km |
| 0 | 625 miles |

Map labels: MEXICO, CENTRAL AMERICA, Mexico City, GUATEMALA, Guatemala City, BELIZE, Belmopan, HONDURAS, Tegucigalpa, San Salvador, EL SALVADOR, NICARAGUA, Managua, COSTA RICA, San Jose, PANAMA, Panama City, Panama Canal, Caracas, VENEZUELA, COLOMBIA, Bogota, GUYANA, Georgetown, SURINAM, Paramaribo, FRENCH GUIANA, Cayenne, Quito, ECUADOR, PERU, Lima, BRAZIL, Brasilia, La Paz, BOLIVIA, PARAGUAY, Asuncion, CHILE, Pacific Ocean, Santiago, URUGUAY, Montevideo, Buenos Aires, ARGENTINA, SOUTH AMERICA, South Atlantic Ocean, FALKLAND ISLANDS, Cape Horn

REVOLUTION IN CUBA

In many Latin American countries, socialism or communism were seen as solutions to instability and poverty. From the 1930s, Cuba was governed by Gulgencio Batista, a corrupt, US-backed dictator. In 1956, a Cuban rebel, named Fidel Castro, joined forces with Che Guevara, an Argentinian

Cuba is only 150km (90 miles) from the USA.

communist who was experienced in guerilla warfare. Together they led rebels against Batista and in 1959 they overthrew him. Castro reformed the government and Cuban society along communist lines. His reforms, backed by the Soviet Union, were successful and brought stability.

Che Guevara became a popular symbol for socialist revolution. His face adorned T-shirts and posters.

ARGENTINA

Argentina earned its living by exporting grain and meat. Then, in the 1930s during the Great Depression, other countries could no longer afford to buy Argentina's produce.

In 1943, a military coup brought the army to power. One of its leaders, Juan Peron, was elected President in 1946. His strong nationalist style gained support from all sections of society. He was deposed in 1955, but returned to power in 1973. In 1976 a harsh new military dictatorship came to power, which lasted until 1983. During this period, in order to stamp out opposition, around 20,000 people were killed.

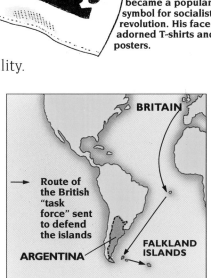

In 1982 Argentina invaded the Falkland Islands, which had been a British colony since 1833. The Argentine invasion force was defeated.

BRAZIL

In the early part of the century, Brazil's coffee exports brought stability and prosperity to the country. In the 1920s, however, social unrest grew and there was a revolt in 1930. In 1964 there was a military takeover, in response to the peasants demanding land reforms.

In 1985 there was a return to elected government, but Brazil still faces many problems. Like the rest of South America, it faces huge debts. There is much social unrest, and environmental problems have been caused by the cutting down of the rainforest.

The destruction of the rainforest. This is one of the world's great environmental problems.

NICARAGUA

In 1933, the wealthy Somoza family came to power in Nicaragua. The peasants were very poor and they supported an opposition group, called the Sandinistas, or FSLN. Frequent clashes led to civil war between 1976-79, in which around 50,000 people were killed.

One of the Sandinista rebels, guerilla fighters who overthrew the government in Nicaragua.

In 1979, the Sandinistas won. They accepted aid from communist countries, which worried the USA because of its business links in Nicaragua. The Contras, an anti-government group, invaded. The US government was later seriously embarrassed when it was revealed that illegal funds had been used to support the Contras. In 1990 peace was agreed, but unrest continued.

FACT BOX

"LATIN" AMERICA

Latin America is an often-used name for the countries in Central and South America. They are so-called because of the influence of Spain and Portugal, which ruled the area until the 1830s. The Spanish and Portuguese languages come from Latin – the ancient language of Rome.

EVA PERON (1919-52)

Juan Peron's wife Eva Peron, known as Evita, was a gifted speaker who spoke out for women's rights. She supported worthy causes which made her popular with the ordinary people. The army stopped her from becoming Vice-President of Argentina and she died of cancer aged 33.

Eva Peron, heroine of the Argentinian people.

FIND OUT MORE

Foreign debt	☞ 45
Argentina	☞ 49
Rainforest	☞ 55

For more information see above pages.

THE COLD WAR

After World War Two, the superpowers grew wary of each other. Both stockpiled nuclear weapons in a "Cold War" – a war of threats and politics, rather than direct conflict.

This Soviet cartoon portrays the West as a ruthless thug.

US poster advertising an anti-communist film.

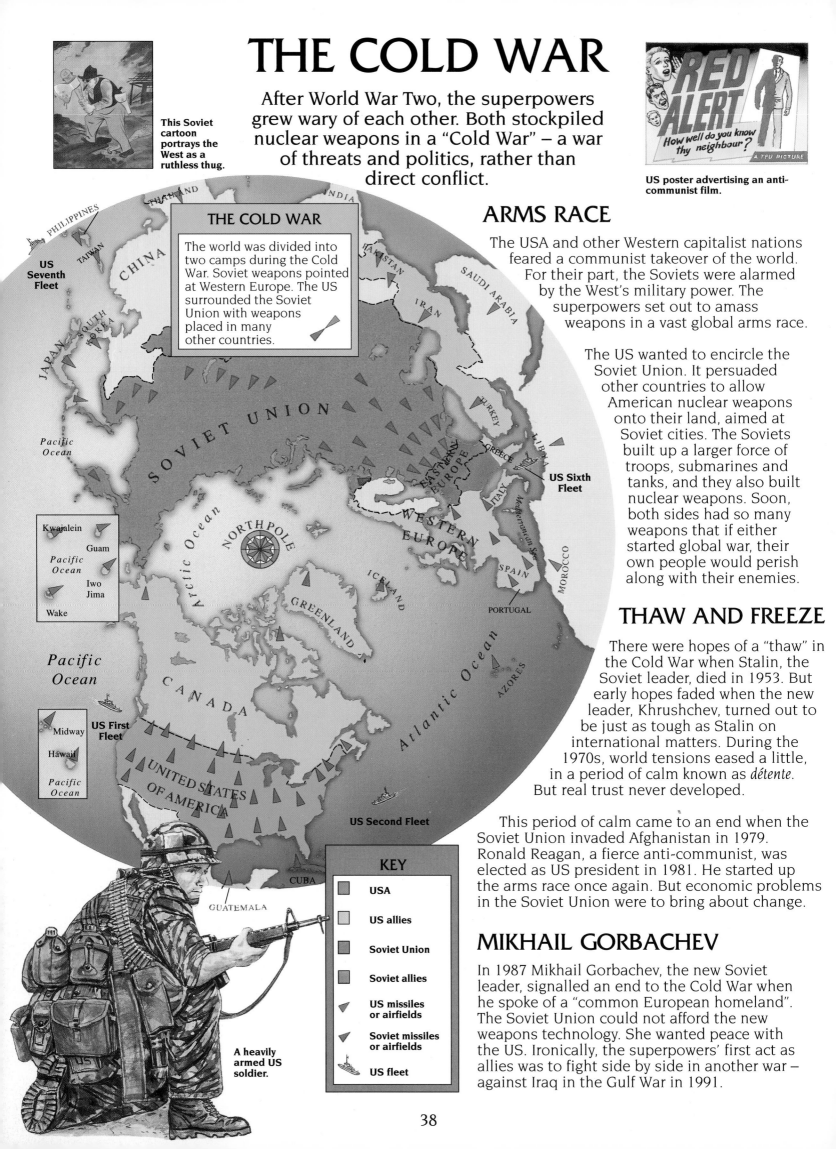

THE COLD WAR

The world was divided into two camps during the Cold War. Soviet weapons pointed at Western Europe. The US surrounded the Soviet Union with weapons placed in many other countries.

ARMS RACE

The USA and other Western capitalist nations feared a communist takeover of the world. For their part, the Soviets were alarmed by the West's military power. The superpowers set out to amass weapons in a vast global arms race.

The US wanted to encircle the Soviet Union. It persuaded other countries to allow American nuclear weapons onto their land, aimed at Soviet cities. The Soviets built up a larger force of troops, submarines and tanks, and they also built nuclear weapons. Soon, both sides had so many weapons that if either started global war, their own people would perish along with their enemies.

THAW AND FREEZE

There were hopes of a "thaw" in the Cold War when Stalin, the Soviet leader, died in 1953. But early hopes faded when the new leader, Khrushchev, turned out to be just as tough as Stalin on international matters. During the 1970s, world tensions eased a little, in a period of calm known as *détente*. But real trust never developed.

This period of calm came to an end when the Soviet Union invaded Afghanistan in 1979. Ronald Reagan, a fierce anti-communist, was elected as US president in 1981. He started up the arms race once again. But economic problems in the Soviet Union were to bring about change.

MIKHAIL GORBACHEV

In 1987 Mikhail Gorbachev, the new Soviet leader, signalled an end to the Cold War when he spoke of a "common European homeland". The Soviet Union could not afford the new weapons technology. She wanted peace with the US. Ironically, the superpowers' first act as allies was to fight side by side in another war – against Iraq in the Gulf War in 1991.

A heavily armed US soldier.

KEY

- USA
- US allies
- Soviet Union
- Soviet allies
- US missiles or airfields
- Soviet missiles or airfields
- US fleet

WORLD WAR OR LOCAL CONFLICT?

Despite their bluffing and threats, in reality the superpowers were anxious to avoid global nuclear war. But each supplied arms to their allies in the Cold War, and sent troops to fight in local conflicts around the world. Often, guerilla fighters outwitted the superpowers' troops, but the fighting caused huge suffering among ordinary people.

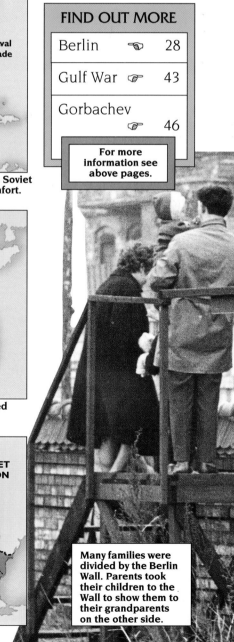

A US nuclear missile. Anti-nuclear protests grew in Europe, where many feared that the superpowers would use nuclear weapons.

KOREA

After Japan's surrender in World War Two, Korea was divided into two halves – Soviet-occupied North Korea and US-occupied South. But when the superpowers withdrew their forces in 1950, both parts of Korea claimed the right to rule the whole country. Border clashes soon began. Communist North Korean troops invaded the south. The US did not want to let Korea become a communist state, so President Truman sent American troops to support South Korean and United Nations forces. After bloody fighting, a peace treaty was agreed in 1953 – but Korea was left divided.

Communist troops invaded South Korea from North Korea.

CUBA

Cuba's new communist leader, Fidel Castro, needed allies. In 1959, the Soviet leader, Khrushchev, offered aid to Cuba – in return for permission to build military bases on the island. In 1963, US spy planes discovered their plans. Swiftly, US President Kennedy ordered a naval blockade of Cuba, threatening to sink any ships which refused to be searched. For days the world teetered on the brink of nuclear war. In the end, Khrushchev backed down. After this terrifying scare, the two superpowers avoided direct conflict. To increase contact, a telephone hotline linked their leaders.

The US blockade of Cuba, where Soviet bases would be too close for comfort.

VIETNAM

In 1963, North Vietnam's communist leader, Ho Chi Minh, launched an invasion of South Vietnam. Worried that nearby China would help to spread communism, the US sent troops to support South Vietnam's dictator. By 1968, 500,000 US troops were struggling in unfamiliar jungle against guerilla fighters. Growing desperate, the Americans sprayed deadly chemicals over villages and farmland. Photos of the war horrified millions in the US, and protests forced the government to withdraw in defeat in 1973. In 1975, North Vietnam united the country under communist rule.

Communist North Vietnam invaded South Vietnam.

EASTERN EUROPE

Eastern Europe was dominated by the Soviet Union. Puppet governments in many nations bowed to Stalin's orders. Even after Stalin's death, Soviet troops crushed a series of anti-communist uprisings in East Germany, Poland, Hungary and Czechoslovakia. The city of Berlin symbolized the East-West split, divided between the Soviet Union and the West since World War Two. In 1961 Soviet and East German troops built the Berlin Wall overnight, to divide the city and stop Eastern Europeans crossing to the West. East German border guards shot people trying to escape.

Revolts were crushed in Poland, Hungary and Czechoslovakia.

FACT BOX

CHINA

At first, communist China was an ally of the Soviet Union. But by 1960 Chinese-Soviet relations had cooled. After this China followed an independent path.

PROPAGANDA

Propaganda means spreading opinions in a one-sided way. Both superpowers used propaganda, such as films and broadcasting, to boost their own system and undermine the other's. Some US politicians stirred up anti-communism. In the 1950s, US Senator Joe McCarthy accused many famous people, such as writers and actors, of being communists. Many people lost their jobs as a result, and some were even sent to prison.

FIND OUT MORE

Berlin	☞	28
Gulf War	☞	43
Gorbachev	☞	46

For more information see above pages.

Many families were divided by the Berlin Wall. Parents took their children to the Wall to show them to their grandparents on the other side.

CHINA – "THE EAST IS RED"

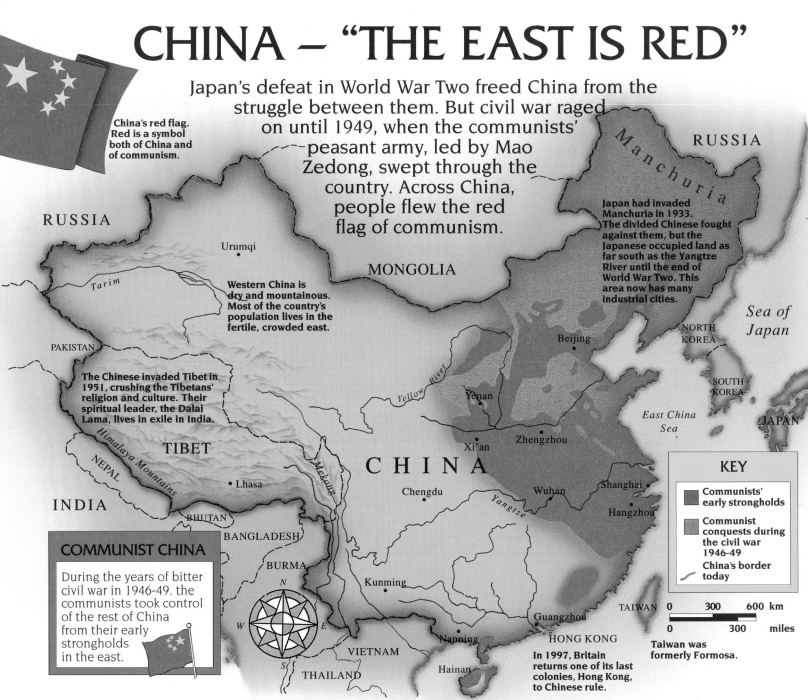

Japan's defeat in World War Two freed China from the struggle between them. But civil war raged on until 1949, when the communists' peasant army, led by Mao Zedong, swept through the country. Across China, people flew the red flag of communism.

China's red flag. Red is a symbol both of China and of communism.

RUSSIA

Urumqi

MONGOLIA

Western China is dry and mountainous. Most of the country's population lives in the fertile, crowded east.

Tarim

PAKISTAN

The Chinese invaded Tibet in 1951, crushing the Tibetans' religion and culture. Their spiritual leader, the Dalai Lama, lives in exile in India.

Himalaya Mountains

NEPAL

TIBET

INDIA

• Lhasa

BHUTAN

BANGLADESH

COMMUNIST CHINA

During the years of bitter civil war in 1946-49, the communists took control of the rest of China from their early strongholds in the east.

BURMA

N
W — E
S

VIETNAM

THAILAND

Mekong

RUSSIA

Manchuria

Japan had invaded Manchuria in 1933. The divided Chinese fought against them, but the Japanese occupied land as far south as the Yangtze River until the end of World War Two. This area now has many industrial cities.

Sea of Japan

Beijing

NORTH KOREA

SOUTH KOREA

Yellow River

Yenan

Xi'an

Zhengzhou

East China Sea

JAPAN

C H I N A

Chengdu

Wuhan

Shanghai •

Hangzhou

Yangtze

Kunming

Guangzhou

Nanning

HONG KONG

Hainan

In 1997, Britain returns one of its last colonies, Hong Kong, to Chinese rule.

KEY

■ Communists' early strongholds

■ Communist conquests during the civil war 1946-49

⌒ China's border today

TAIWAN

0 _____ 300 _____ 600 km

0 _____ 300 _____ miles

Taiwan was formerly Formosa.

THE NEW STATE

China's hundreds of millions of peasants were poor, overworked and hungry. They welcomed the communists, who offered them peace, land reform and education. In 1949, Mao and the communist government set about building up China's industry and economy, ravaged by decades of war. They took land away from the landlords and gave it to the peasants. The peasants were keen to work on their own small plots of land, but few wanted to live and work on the large collective farms planned by the communists.

中国

东方红

The communists simplified Chinese writing, to make it easier to learn to read and write. This says "China – the East is Red".

FIVE YEAR PLAN

Mao's first Five Year Plan, begun in 1953, achieved mixed results. Factories met their vast orders – but produced shoddy goods. There was unrest in the countryside as peasants were forced onto collective farms, or communes.

In response, Mao launched a new campaign in 1957 inviting people to discuss the way forward. It was called "Let a Hundred Flowers Bloom". People entered the new debate with enthusiasm. But many who criticized the Communist Party were punished. Some thought they had been tricked into speaking out. Mao had shown himself to be a strong, ruthless leader.

GREAT LEAP FORWARD

In 1958, Mao announced the Great Leap Forward. He saw steel as the key to industrial growth. Tiny "backyard furnaces" were to double steel production every year. All peasants were to work on huge communes. But the results were disastrous. No crops were sown, and in the countryside millions died of famine. Mountains of brittle steel had to be scrapped.

"Backyard furnaces" like this one were powered by hand. To meet orders for steel, people melted down their own metal pots and pans.

CULTURAL REVOLUTION

Mao wanted permanent revolution, to stop people from growing complacent. In 1967 he launched the Cultural Revolution. He called on the young to rise up and criticize their elders, especially intellectuals and old-fashioned communist party members. Many pupils accused teachers of anti-revolutionary thoughts, and some children even reported their parents. Millions were beaten, tortured or driven to suicide. Schools were closed and factories stopped work. Normal life was impossible. Troops sent to calm the violence and chaos joined in the fighting. At last, by 1968, order was restored, but only by clamping down severely on people's freedom. Millions lost their education when Mao ordered young people to go to work in the fields, to learn from the peasants.

During the Cultural Revolution, young people answered Mao's call to arms. Battalions of fanatical teenagers, called Red Guards, terrorized the cities.

FINAL DAYS OF MAO

By the 1970s, Mao was growing old and sick. His wife and her supporters, known as the Gang of Four, plotted ruthlessly to hang onto power. But by 1973, Deng Xiaoping and Chou En Lai had taken over day to day governing. They started to dismantle the Cultural Revolution. When Mao died in 1976, the Gang of Four were tried and imprisoned for their brutal crimes.

Mao Zedong, China's leader from 1948 to 1976.

THE "NEW CHINA"

Deng wanted to reform China's economy and scrap the communes. He sought Western and Japanese help to modernize China's backward industry. This meant admitting that Mao had made disastrous mistakes in his later years.

Deng's reforms worked. By the early 1980s, factories were flourishing with the new investment, and farmers produced far more crops. Deng encouraged trade and built links with tiny, prosperous Hong Kong, in preparation for her return to Chinese rule.

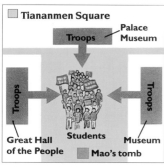

☆ Democracy protests

CHINA Beijing
Lanzhou
Xi'an Hefei
Nanjing
Wuhan
Chengdu

In 1989, democracy protests spread quickly across China. Demonstrations erupted in many cities, often led by students.

TIANANMEN SQUARE MASSACRE

By the late 1980s, the people grew impatient for change, especially after *glasnost* reforms in the Soviet Union. In April 1989, Beijing students began to demand democracy. Protests spread across China. In May, half a million people demonstrated in Beijing's Tiananmen Square to support the three thousand students on hunger strike there.

Deng's hardline prime minister, Li Peng, called in the army. On June 4th, 1989, troops massacred up to a thousand students in Tiananmen Square. Thousands more were imprisoned or executed. The Chinese people's call for democracy remains denied.

☐ Tiananmen Square
Palace Museum
Troops
Troops
Troops
Students
Great Hall of the People
Museum
☐ Mao's tomb

Troops surrounded the protestors camping in Tiananmen Square. Tanks drove through the capital's streets to enter the square.

This young man bravely stood in front of a line of tanks to stop them from entering Tiananmen Square. He was taken away by police.

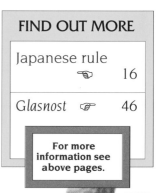

THE MIDDLE EAST

After Israel was formed in 1948, conflict over land and religion exploded into war again and again in the Middle East. Rival Arab states, united by hatred of Israel, used oil wealth to buy arms and support terrorists. Islamic and Jewish extremists resisted peaceful compromise.

This extremist Palestinian poster says "Smash Israel".

A supporter holds up a portrait of the *Ayatollah* Khomeini, Iran's Islamic leader from 1979-89.

ISRAEL

The new state of Israel was supported in 1948 by both the USA and the Soviet Union. In America, Jewish groups pressed the US government to send aid and arms to Israel. At first the Soviet Union was pleased to see Israel's new socialist government and the communist-style farms, or *kibbutzim*, which produced most of Israel's food. But gradually the Soviets turned against the new state. As the Cold War developed, they counter-balanced US support for Israel by sending tanks and fighter planes to several Arab nations.

Israel was tiny – only 15km (9 miles) across at her narrowest point – and surrounded by hostile nations. She felt vulnerable. But her defiant military response and treatment of the Palestinians led to criticism from the rest of the world.

ISRAEL AND THE ARAB STATES

Israel won extra land in the Six Day War of 1967. Many Palestinian Arabs lived in the areas taken by Israel. Since 1995 some of these Palestinian areas have won self-rule after lengthy peace negotiations.

ARAB-ISRAELI WARS

Between 1956 and 1973 Israel and the Arab nations fought three wars. The Arabs vowed to destroy the new state, force out the Jews and set up a Palestinian state in its place. Colonel Nasser, Egypt's strong new leader, united Arab nations behind him.

Israel was constantly on guard against attack. In a war lasting just six days, in 1967, the Israelis won strategically important land. This increased their feeling of security. Jewish extremists claimed that this land should always be part of Israel, and they built settlements there. But the many Palestinian Arabs in the area did not want to live under Israeli rule.

In October 1977, after months of secret talks, Egypt shocked the world when her next leader, President Sadat, signed a peace treaty with Israel. As part of the peace deal, Israel handed Sinai back to Egypt. Arab extremists assassinated Sadat in 1981.

Golda Meir, Israel's Prime Minister from 1969 to 1974.

THE OIL CRISIS

Middle Eastern countries exported oil to many Western nations, who came to rely upon it. In 1960, these countries, united by their religion (Islam), formed a trading group called OPEC*. OPEC was hostile to Israel. In 1973, the Arab nations lost the Yom Kippur War against Israel. OPEC members decided to reduce oil supplies to Israel's supporters, including the US, until they withdrew their support. The cost of oil increased by five times in a year, causing economic crisis in the West. But still Israel clung to the land she had won in 1967.

*Organization of Petroleum Exporting Countries

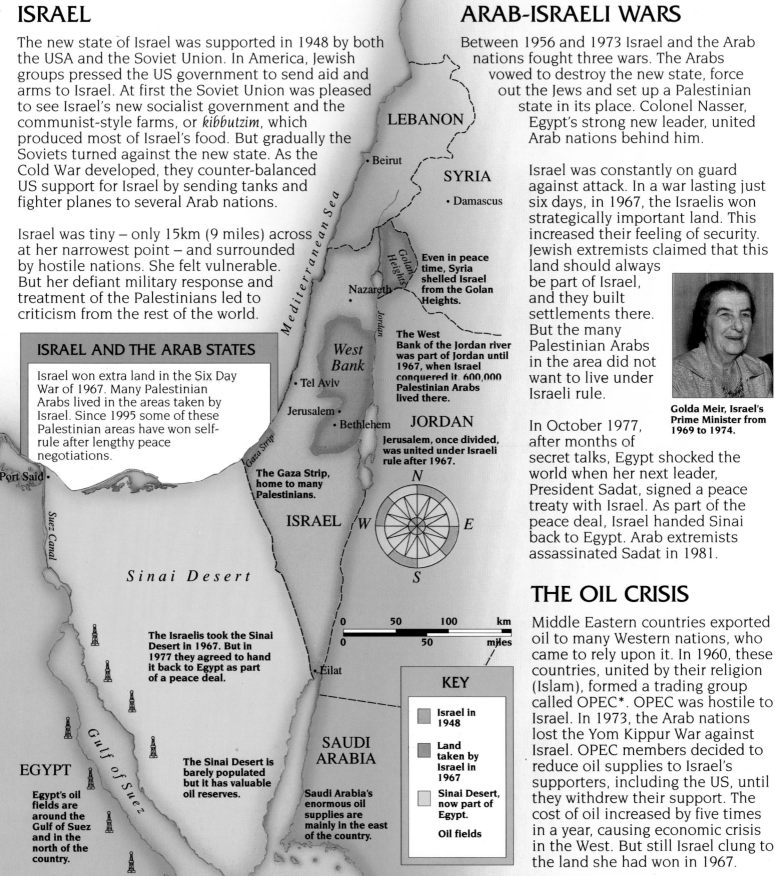

Mediterranean Sea

LEBANON

• Beirut

SYRIA

• Damascus

Golan Heights

Even in peace time, Syria shelled Israel from the Golan Heights.

Nazareth •

Jordan

The West Bank of the Jordan river was part of Jordan until 1967, when Israel conquered it. 600,000 Palestinian Arabs lived there.

West Bank

• Tel Aviv

Jerusalem •
• Bethlehem

JORDAN

Jerusalem, once divided, was united under Israeli rule after 1967.

Gaza Strip

The Gaza Strip, home to many Palestinians.

ISRAEL

N
W E
S

Port Said •

Suez Canal

Sinai Desert

The Israelis took the Sinai Desert in 1967. But in 1977 they agreed to hand it back to Egypt as part of a peace deal.

| 0 | 50 | 100 | km |

| 0 | 50 | | miles |

• Eilat

EGYPT

Egypt's oil fields are around the Gulf of Suez and in the north of the country.

Gulf of Suez

The Sinai Desert is barely populated but it has valuable oil reserves.

SAUDI ARABIA

Saudi Arabia's enormous oil supplies are mainly in the east of the country.

KEY

■ Israel in 1948

■ Land taken by Israel in 1967

□ Sinai Desert, now part of Egypt.

⛏ Oil fields

Red Sea

PALESTINIAN ANGER

Since the formation of Israel, hundreds of thousands of Palestinians had lived in squalid refugee camps in Arab countries. There they were denied citizenship, homes and freedom. In 1964, a new movement was formed, called the Palestinian Liberation Organization, or PLO. Its leader was Yassir Arafat. In the 1970s, supported by Arab nations, the PLO carried out terrorist attacks to draw attention to their cause. In 1987, Palestinians inside Israel launched a violent uprising, or *Intifada*, to call for independence. Thousands of young men were exiled, imprisoned or killed in street fighting over the next few years.

Palestinian refugee camps were mostly in Lebanon and on the West Bank of the Jordan river. The West Bank became a part of Israel in 1967.

THE LEBANON

Lebanon, on Israel's northern border, was home to many rival groups. Tensions exploded in a complex and bloody civil war in 1975 between different Islamic groups, Christians, Syrian fighters, and the PLO, whose headquarters were based there. The capital, Beirut, was reduced to rubble. In response to shelling over her borders, in 1982 Israel invaded southern Lebanon, hoping to drive out Palestinian terrorists and create a neutral buffer zone along her border. The world protested against Israeli aggression, and her troops withdrew in 1983. But this did not put an end to fighting in Lebanon.

During the Lebanese civil war, a strip of wasteland called the "Green Line" divided the capital, Beirut, into the Muslim west and the Christian east.

IRAN, IRAQ AND KUWAIT

In 1979, the King or *Shah* of Iran was overthrown by a fiercely anti-Western group of Islamic religious leaders. In 1980, Iraq's dictator, Saddam Hussein, declared war on Iran. The West supplied Iraq with weapons, hoping to stop the spread of extremist Islamic feeling in the Middle East. The war dragged on for eight years, and millions died. Having failed to crush Iran, in 1990 Iraq invaded Kuwait. This threatened Saudi Arabia – and the West's oil supplies. The UN acted swiftly. In the Gulf War, as it was called, the Americans led international troops against Iraqi forces, bombing them into surrender.

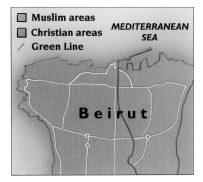

Saddam Hussein's army, the fourth largest in the world, invaded Kuwait in 1990 – only two years after the long war with Iran ended without a clear winner.

SHALOM, SALAAM – PEACE

After the Gulf War, many Palestinians decided on a more moderate approach. Yasser Arafat led peace talks with Israel. These negotiations were long and difficult, and brought protests from both Jewish and Arab extremists. Spring 1996 saw the first elections for self-rule in Palestinian areas inside Israel. But doubts remain on both sides. In 1995, Israeli Prime Minister Rabin was assassinated by an extremist Jew.

Yitzhak Rabin (left) and Yasser Arafat (right) make peace in 1993. US President Clinton congratulates them.

DEVELOPING WORLD

Simple wells like this can provide clean drinking water.

Most nations in Africa and Asia won independence from European rule in the years after World War Two. Many are now known as developing countries because their farming and industry are not yet as developed as those in the industrialized world.

Aung San Suu Kyi, elected as leader by the people of Burma.

FREEDOM AND HOPE

After independence, people had high hopes of freedom, democracy and wealth. In many countries, though, European rule left behind poverty, and recovery has been slow. Many new nations have been plagued by corrupt governments, civil wars, poverty and famine, so most people are no wealthier than they were before.

Richer countries sent aid but did little to tackle the causes of poverty in the developing world, such as trading disadvantages. Many developing countries still struggle to provide basic services such as health care and education for their fast-growing populations.

DICTATORS

One of the main problems to face many developing countries after independence was the rise of dictators – leaders who rule alone and have absolute control over people's lives.

A terrible example was Cambodia in the 1970s and 80s. By 1975, Pol Pot, leader of the Khmer Rouge (the Cambodian Communist Party), had taken control of the country. Around two and a half million Cambodians, nearly half the population, died during his reign of terror. In 1993, elections excluded the Khmer Rouge from power, but guerilla fighting continued after this.

PEOPLE'S HEROES

The struggle for freedom from dictatorship has brought forth some heroic leaders. One example is Aung San Suu Kyi of Burma. Since 1962, Burma has been in the grip of harsh military dictators who have renamed it Myanmar.

Even though Aung San Suu Kyi led the National League for Democracy to victory in elections in 1990, she has not been allowed to govern. Since then, she has lived under house arrest and has not been able to see her family. Each week, people gather outside her home, risking imprisonment to hear her speak.

AFTER THE EMPIRES FELL

Shared language or religion can bind people together into cultural groups. European rule had held varied cultural groups together, often ignoring their differences. After independence, many peoples wanted self-rule. Some have demanded the right to break away and form an independent state.

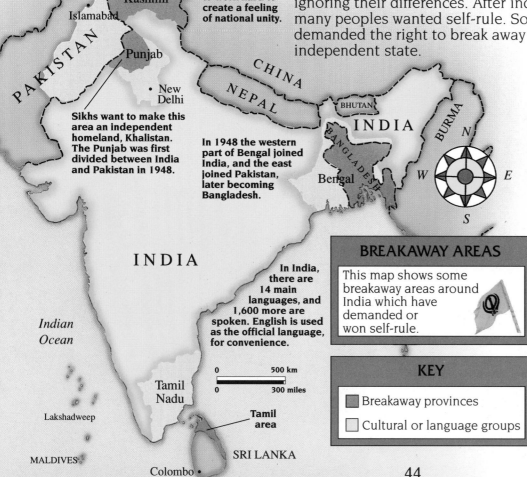

India is a country of many languages and religions. It has to work hard to create a feeling of national unity.

Sikhs want to make this area an independent homeland, Khalistan. The Punjab was first divided between India and Pakistan in 1948.

In 1948 the western part of Bengal joined India, and the east joined Pakistan, later becoming Bangladesh.

In India, there are 14 main languages, and 1,600 more are spoken. English is used as the official language, for convenience.

0	500 km
0	300 miles

BREAKAWAY AREAS

This map shows some breakaway areas around India which have demanded or won self-rule.

KEY

Breakaway provinces
Cultural or language groups

Tamil area

The Sikh flag. Sikhs want a homeland in the Punjab.

In 1948, when India and the Islamic state of Pakistan won independence, the area of Bengal was divided between them. Many people fled from one side to the other. Eastern Bengal became East Pakistan and was ruled from the main part of Pakistan. In 1971, it won self-rule, and was renamed Bangladesh.

Jammu and Kashmir, one of India's few Islamic regions, wants its independence. India and Pakistan have fought for control of the area.

Thousands of Tamils, Hindu people originally from the province of Tamil Nadu in southern India, have lived in Sri Lanka for centuries. Now they want their own state. In northeast Sri Lanka, guerillas called the Tamil Tigers are fighting a bitter civil war.

FAMINE

Developing countries have suffered devastating famines when severe drought causes crops to fail, and land turns into desert. Often famine is also caused by war. In Ethiopia in the 1980s, for instance, 800,000 people died in a terrible famine. Food was available, including aid sent from abroad, but soldiers fighting in the civil war stopped trucks from taking it to enemy parts of the country.

TRADE AND AID

In the 1960s and 70s, rich nations sent aid in the form of loans to developing countries, to help them build up their industry. Many developing countries are now struggling to repay the loans and the charges for borrowing. To earn cash, they have to grow crops to sell abroad, such as coffee or cotton, instead of food for their people. But developing countries are disadvantaged over trade, too. Industrialized countries keep down prices for the raw materials. Then they use these to manufacture goods such as instant coffee, which sell for more profit.

SMALL-SCALE AID

In 1985, during Ethiopia's famine, a huge televised pop concert called Live Aid raised $70,000,000 to send food to the starving. Aid organizations also support small-scale projects which help people to become self-sufficient and skilled. In the long term it is more useful to train people in tree planting to stop soil erosion, for instance, than to send food or fund high-tech projects which are hard to mend if they break down.

A NEW PATH

In 1991, Eritrea broke free from Ethiopia after 30 years of war. The new nation is determined to rebuild itself without using costly international loans. Instead, the people work by hand to clear fields and build roads, rather than using expensive machinery. Old trains, built by Italian colonizers in the 1930s, are being carefully restored and brought back into service.

Deserts around the world are growing, increasing the risk of famine. One cause is overgrazing by cattle and goats, bred to try to produce more food for the rising population. This can leave the soil bare and in danger of blowing away, called soil erosion.

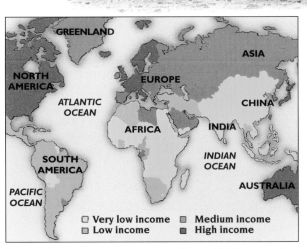

Average income per person around the world. The poorest countries are in Africa and Asia.

- □ Very low income
- □ Low income
- ■ Medium income
- ■ High income

This woman has used a small loan from the Grameen Bank to buy a rickshaw and start her own business for her family.

COMMUNISM FALLS

People waved the Romanian flag with the communist symbol ripped out.

Communist control in Eastern Europe ended with a peaceful revolution. Except in Romania, hardly a shot was fired. Many different peoples have won self-rule at last. But for some, the new freedom has brought uncertainty and chaos.

Eastern Europeans driving to the West after the fall of communism.

GORBACHEV

Mikhail Gorbachev came to power in the Soviet Union in 1985. He admitted that the nation was facing industrial and economic failure, made worse by the long, unpopular war with Afghanistan. Gorbachev swiftly drew up plans for change, and withdrew from Afghanistan. He soon grabbed the goodwill of the public, as a young, energetic leader who wanted to improve people's lives.

Mikhail Gorbachev, the leader who dismantled the Soviet Union.

REFORM

Gorbachev launched a series of reforms, called *perestroika*. People could now vote in free elections, and set up their own businesses. *Glasnost*, or openness, meant more honest reporting of problems, such as the shortages of everyday goods in the shops. Past failings were revealed, including the horrors of Stalin's rule. At first, people were delighted with the new freedoms. But soon they became impatient for more change.

PERESTROIKA ABROAD

At the seventieth anniversary celebrations of the Russian Revolution, in 1987, Gorbachev encouraged other communist leaders to reform too. Some welcomed his message enthusiastically. More traditional leaders, such as East Germany's Erich Honecker, were furious. Gorbachev's words sent a signal that Soviet troops would not crush anti-communist protests as they had in the past. As a result, people all over Eastern Europe began to demand free elections. This encouraged an exciting new feeling of independence among peoples of many different cultures.

AFTER COMMUNISM

The vast communist empire broke up in the late 1980s. Many new nations rose out of it. Other peoples of the old Soviet Union joined together to form the Russian Federation.

KEY

— Boundary of the old Soviet Union

Nations now independent of the Soviet Union

Areas of self-rule by ethnic groups within the Russian Federation

Formerly communist countries of Eastern Europe

✶✶ Former Iron Curtain

In many regions, most of the population is not Russian, but belongs to other ethnic groups. Many now have self-rule, but still belong to the Russian Federation.

Conflict has arisen in many parts of the former Soviet Union. Control over valuable oil supplies in the southwest has triggered tension.

CANADA

Arctic Ocean

GREENLAND

ICELAND

North Sea

Atlantic Ocean

SIBERIA

Lena

Ural Mountains

Ob

NORWAY

SWEDEN

FINLAND

ESTONIA

LATVIA

LITHUANIA

Baltic Sea

IRELAND BRITAIN

DENMARK

NETHER-LANDS

BELGIUM

GERMANY

RUSSIAN FED.

POLAND

BELARUS

RUSSIAN FEDERATION

KAZAKHSTAN

EUROPE

FRANCE

SWITZERLAND

AUSTRIA

SLOVAKIA

HUNGARY

CZECH REPUBLIC

UKRAINE

MOLDOVA

ITALY

SLOVENIA

CROATIA

BOSNIA

YUGOSLAVIA

ROMANIA

SPAIN

Mediterranean Sea

MACEDONIA

ALBANIA

GREECE

BULGARIA

Black Sea

GEORGIA

ARMENIA

AZERBAIJAN

Caspian Sea

Aral Sea

UZBEKISTAN

TURKMENISTAN

KYRGYZSTAN

TAJIKISTAN

Himalaya Mountains

ASIA

SOVIET DISUNION

In 1990 Lithuania, Latvia and Estonia declared themselves independent from the Soviet Union. The call for self-rule spread, bringing fighting in some places. People grew impatient for still more change. After a failed coup against him, Gorbachev stepped down, and Boris Yeltsin became president in his place. On December 31, 1991, the Soviet Union was declared at an end. In the new economic system, some have grown wealthy. But the cost of food and fuel has risen, and life is harder for many, especially old people with small pensions. Some people miss the old certainties of communism.

This Soviet poster says "Long live peace among all the peoples". For decades, the Soviet Union had held together many different peoples, who split apart when the union broke up.

Many monuments to communist heroes, like this statue of Lenin, were demolished after communism fell.

EASTERN EUROPE THROWS OFF COMMUNISM

East Germany was freed from communist control in May 1989 when Hungary opened its Austrian border. The East German leader, Erich Honecker, condemned this move, but thousands grasped the chance to go to the West. Many visited relatives they had not seen for decades. In November 1989, Germans on both sides of the hated Berlin Wall rejoiced as it was torn down. East Germans could now travel freely for the first time. The two Germanies were reunited less than a year later. Now Germans are working hard to make the poorer eastern regions as efficient and wealthy as the West.

When Hungary opened its Austrian border, East Germans came through Czechoslovakia to the West.

Poland was the first to rise against communism. In 1979, striking ship workers formed an anti-communist trade union, Solidarity. Communist army leaders passed strict laws, but Solidarity continued to grow and in 1989 won a huge election victory.

In Czechoslovakia, the mass demonstrations that brought about change were so peaceful that they were known as the Velvet Revolution. In 1992 the country split peacefully into two independent halves – the Czech Republic and Slovakia.

Protests in Romania began in 1989, while Ceaucescu, the brutal dictator, was away. He returned to address a demonstration, but the people refused to hear him speak. He fled, but was captured and executed – the only communist leader to die.

National feeling grew in Poland when the new Polish Pope, John Paul II, visited the capital, Warsaw, in 1979. Major demonstrations took place at Gdansk, Poznan and Katowice.

Mass protests in Brno and the capital, Prague, in 1989 brought change in Czechoslovakia. The Czechs and Slovaks, thrown together after World War One, have now split.

Romanian protests started in Timisoara, after the arrest of a priest who stood up for the Hungarian minority. Unrest soon spread to the capital, Bucharest.

FACT BOX

COMMUNISM LIVES

Not all communist governments lost power in 1989-91. China resisted students' demands for democracy in 1989. Communist governments in Albania, Vietnam, Cuba and North Korea still have some popular support.

LECH WALESA

Lech Walesa, a Gdansk electrician, set up the Polish trade union, Solidarity, in 1980, and was awarded the Nobel Peace Prize in 1983. In 1990 Walesa was elected President of Poland.

MIKHAIL GORBACHEV

As a child during World War Two, Mikhail Gorbachev survived the German occupation of his village near the Black Sea. He worked on the land and then trained as a lawyer. He wanted to modernize communism to make it popular once again.

CHERNOBYL

In 1986, a huge explosion at a nuclear power station in Chernobyl, Ukraine, blew radioactive dust across Europe. Illnesses caused by radiation have claimed many lives there. Although the news was reported internationally, it was not until after the *glasnost* reforms that the full details were reported to the Soviet people.

EUROPEAN UNION

Many former communist states want to join the European Union (EU), in the hope of economic growth. Western European members of the EU have made a show of welcoming them, but are worried that they will be costly to support.

The EU grew out of the European Community (formerly the Common Market). Members vote at its joint parliament on economics and other shared issues. In 1993, the Maastricht Treaty drew members into closer union. In the future, the EU may take on even wider powers in member states.

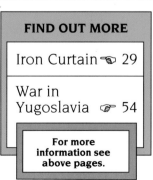

For more information see above pages.

WOMEN TODAY

During the twentieth century, women have fought for the right to vote and for education, careers and birth control. Many women today have more freedom than their mothers or grandmothers.

During both world wars, governments asked women to take over men's jobs. This poster encouraged British women to do war work.

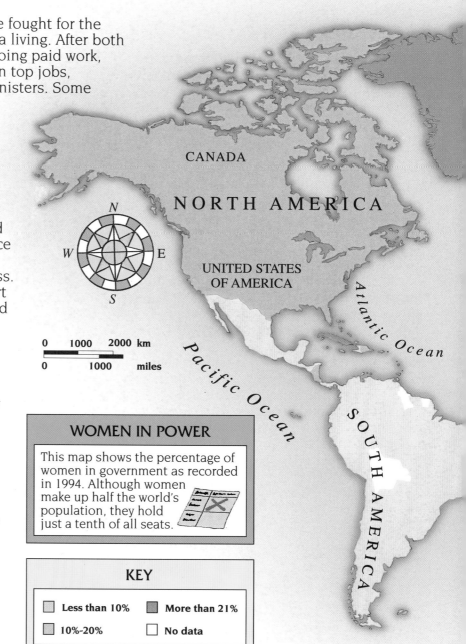

This suffragette is led away from a demonstration calling for votes for women in Britain before World War One.

SUFFRAGETTES

By 1900, women could vote in national elections only in New Zealand and Australia. In Britain and the USA, women protestors known as suffragettes organized huge demonstrations to demand the vote. Some even went to prison where they went on hunger strike to draw attention to their cause. During World War One, millions of women worked in the factories and fields. In 1918, in recognition of their work, British women over 30 won the vote. Two years later, so did women over 21 in the USA.

WOMEN AND WORK

Throughout the twentieth century, women have fought for the freedom and independence gained by earning a living. After both world wars, many women wanted to carry on doing paid work, rather than stay at home. Women began to gain top jobs, becoming managers, judges or government ministers. Some churches and synagogues now ordain women priests and rabbis. But progress is slow. Despite laws on equal pay, in many countries women still earn much less than men.

WOMEN'S CAMPAIGNS

Around the world, women in action groups and trade unions have campaigned for peace, justice and equal rights. Often they use peaceful, untraditional tactics to get their message across. In many developing countries, women took part in the struggle against colonial rule. They called for women's rights to be a part of the new freedom of independence.

A handful of women, such as Mrs. Sirimavo Bandaranaike of Sri Lanka, have been elected as prime ministers. But there is still a long way to go before women and men are elected to government in equal numbers.

In 1960, Mrs. Bandaranaike of Sri Lanka became the first woman in the world to be elected Prime Minister.

CANADA

NORTH AMERICA

UNITED STATES OF AMERICA

Atlantic Ocean

Pacific Ocean

SOUTH AMERICA

0   1000   2000 km

0   1000   miles

WOMEN IN POWER

This map shows the percentage of women in government as recorded in 1994. Although women make up half the world's population, they hold just a tenth of all seats.

KEY

Less than 10%   More than 21%

10%-20%   No data

48

BIRTH CONTROL

Without birth control (which lets people plan if or when they have children) women might have up to a dozen children. This means that they would spend most of their time and energy caring for children. Improved methods of birth control let women choose to have a small family, leaving them more time for activities outside the home as well.

In developing countries with poor health care, many women continue to have large families because so many children die from malnutrition and disease. Until parents can be fairly sure that their children will survive, many will be reluctant to use birth control. Some Catholic and Islamic leaders discourage birth control for religious reasons.

An early clinic offering birth control to mothers in the 1920s.

FEMINISM

Feminism is a movement which calls for women to have the same rights and freedom as men. The feminist movement grew up in Europe and the USA in the 1960s and 70s. It built on the achievements of the suffragettes and other women who campaigned early in the twentieth century for better education for girls, and improved working conditions for women.

Feminists now campaign for fair pay and working conditions, more childcare and for health care which meets women's needs. They also demand punishment for men who commit violent crimes against women and children.

WOMEN ACHIEVERS

IDA B. WELLS-BARNETT
Ida Wells-Barnett (1862-1931) campaigned in the USA for justice against vicious lynch mobs, who murdered black people. She helped to set up the National Association for the Advancement of Colored People in 1909.

MARIE STOPES
Marie Stopes (1880-1958) believed that women should be able to use birth control. Despite protests from doctors and Christian groups, she set up the first clinic in London offering birth control to women.

COCO CHANEL
Coco Chanel (1883-1971) was a fashion designer. Early in the twentieth century she designed comfortable, stylish dresses in soft fabrics such as wool and flannel, which liberated women from tight, painful corsets.

AMELIA EARHART
Amelia Earhart (1898-1937) was a pioneer American aviator. In 1932 she became the first woman to fly solo across the Atlantic. She died when her plane was lost without trace on the last leg of a trip around the world.

MOTHER TERESA
Mother Teresa, born in 1910, trained as a nun. She set up a worldwide charity caring for orphans, drug addicts and victims of famine and civil war.

VALENTINA TERESHKOVA
Valentina Tereshkova, born in 1937, was the first woman astronaut to fly in space. In 1963 she piloted Soviet spacecraft Vostok 6 for 48 orbits of the Earth.

At 39%, Finland has the highest proportion of women in parliament.

In the 1980s, women set up peace camps outside US army bases in Europe, in protest at nuclear weapons stationed there.

SCANDINAVIA

RUSSIA

EUROPE

ASIA

MIDDLE EAST

AFRICA

CHINA

Pacific Ocean

Mrs. Indira Gandhi was elected three times as Prime Minister of India, first of all in 1966.

A few small countries, such as Papua New Guinea, have no women yet in their governments.

Indian Ocean

In South Africa, women of all races fought against apartheid. They set up schools for black children and organized boycotts and strikes.

In some Islamic countries, for instance in the Middle East, spiritual leaders dictate how women dress, and whether or not they can work. Many women have argued that true Islam should not oppress women.

AUSTRALIA

NEW ZEALAND

In Argentina, in South America, the mothers of people murdered by the military government in the 1970s bravely protested every week in the capital. Up to 20,000 people were killed, known as "the Disappeared".

APARICION CON VIDA

Mothers of the Disappeared wearing white headscarves at a protest against the murder of their children. Their banner demands "openness" or truth about their fate.

RIGHTS FOR EVERYONE

One of the greatest changes to take place in the twentieth century is the rise in democracy (the right to vote). Kings and queens no longer have absolute say and great empires no longer rule the world.

A wheelchair athlete. In fairer societies, those with disabilities now have the chance of a freer life and to enjoy activities once denied them.

A RISE IN DEMOCRACY

In 1900, in most countries of the world, few men and even fewer women had the right to vote. Now, many countries of the world are democratic and more people than ever before are able to have a say in how their country is run. Even the old Soviet Union saw itself as democratic, because people could vote within the Communist Party. This is also true of modern day China. This rise in democracy has encouraged people to campaign against injustices that they feel are neglected by their governments.

Democracy has inspired people to campaign for change. The organization Amnesty International campaigns for people imprisoned for their beliefs.

The Campaign for Nuclear Disarmament protested against nuclear weapons.

UNICEF, a branch of the United Nations, works on behalf of child welfare around the world.

GREENPEACE

Greenpeace campaigns for the protection of endangered species and the environment.

THE JARROW MARCH

During the Great Depression, unemployment was desperately high in the industrialized world. Many popular protests took place against the poverty in which the working class found themselves. One such protest took place in 1936. Two hundred and seven unemployed men from Jarrow, a shipbuilding town in northeast England, went on a march to London. They carried a petition to the government protesting about unemployment in their town.

Jarrow (near Newcastle upon Tyne)
Leeds
Route of the Jarrow March
BRITAIN
London

The men walked 480km (300 miles) from Jarrow to London with their petition in October 1936.

CIVIL RIGHTS IN THE USA

In the 1950s, a campaign for equal rights for black people, known as the Civil Rights Movement, surfaced in the USA. In 1954, after a legal battle, it was announced that segregated schools (in which the different races were taught separately) were against the law. Desegregation of schools followed, but in some areas, especially the southern states, there was fierce opposition.

Civil Rights Acts were passed to enforce equality, and peaceful protests were held to force desegregation. One of the leaders of the Civil Rights Movement was a Baptist minister called Martin Luther King. He was awarded the Nobel Peace Prize in 1964, but was assassinated four years later while on a civil rights mission in Memphis, Tennessee. Despite more Civil Rights Acts, many people believe that there is still widespread prejudice.

Martin Luther King, one of the leaders of the Civil Rights Movement in the USA.

In the 1960s, people in the United States protested against the Vietnam War. Here, peace demonstrators are held back by military police.

UNITED STATES OF AMERICA
Famous march on Washington 1963
Born (1929), lived and worked in Atlanta
Assassinated in Memphis 1968
Led his first protests in Montgomery 1955
The southern states

Major events in King's life. The southern states were traditionally against civil rights for blacks.

THE RIGHT TO LAND AND CULTURE

One of the major injustices in today's world is the situation of many of the indigenous peoples (original inhabitants) of Australasia and America. When white settlers arrived, they lost their land, culture and way of life and many found it impossible to fit into a new society. Their numbers fell rapidly and many were reduced to living in squalor and misery.

ABORIGINES

In Australia, many Aborigine people were killed by settlers, who regarded their culture as inferior. Since the 1930s there have been campaigns to give them more rights and they were granted the right to vote in 1967. Aborigines are determined to preserve their culture, history and land rights. They have made demands to share the wealth earned from mining in Aboriginal regions.

An Aborigine playing the didgeridoo – a traditional instrument.

AUSTRALASIA

Together, Australia and New Zealand are known as Australasia. Tasmania is part of Australia.

MAORIS

In New Zealand, the indigenous people are the Maoris. In 1929, the Young Maori Party managed to win more rights with the Native Land Settlement Act. This provided Maoris with money and land to develop their traditional culture. The Ratana political movement and the New Zealand Labour Party have campaigned for reforms and promoted an awareness of Maori culture, although there are still disagreements over land ownership.

The Maoris see themselves as linked culturally with the Polynesians of the Pacific islands, to the east.

GREAT SANDY DESERT

AUSTRALIA

Vast regions of Australia are uninhabited, dry land, known as the Outback.

Brisbane

Lake Eyre

Cooper's Creek

Perth

Sydney

Adelaide

Murray

Canberra

Melbourne

PACIFIC OCEAN

Auckland

Wellington

NEW ZEALAND

TASMANIA

Hobart

KEY

- Aboriginal land, given to the Aborigines by the Australian government
- The Outback

0	1000	km
0	625	miles

AMERICAN INDIANS

By the late nineteenth century, North American Indians were defeated by the US army and confined to areas called reservations. In 1924, they gained full citizenship, but their status in society was slow to improve.

To protect South American Indians from a similiar fate, people are campaigning to protect their way of life. But they are under constant threat from developers closing in on their rainforest homes.

CANADA

UNITED STATES OF AMERICA

Indian reservation

Reservations in North America. Many Indians still live there, but have protested about conditions.

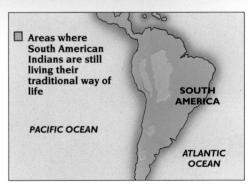

Areas where South American Indians are still living their traditional way of life

SOUTH AMERICA

PACIFIC OCEAN

ATLANTIC OCEAN

Areas of South America where Indians live. Around 100 groups have been wiped out since 1900.

FACT BOX

"I HAVE A DREAM"

In 1963, Martin Luther King led over 200,000 people in a peaceful Civil Rights march through the streets of Washington. At the Lincoln Memorial, the march ended and King made a famous speech. He said, "I have a dream that my four little children will be judged not by the color of their skin, but by the content of their character."

CHILDREN'S RIGHTS

In many developing countries, young children work in conditions which are little better than slavery. Despite long hours and dangerous surroundings, they earn a pittance. In wealthy countries, the hours and conditions in which children work are strictly regulated, but some are still at risk from cruelty and abuse by adults.

CENTURY OF SCIENCE

Marie Curie (1867-1934) discovered radium, used to treat cancer.

During the twentieth century, science and technology have transformed everyday life – in industrialized countries at least. They have also generated deadly weapons. Now the challenge for science is to bring peaceful progress to the whole planet.

The shuttle uses its robot arm to launch this satellite.

The satellite will carry out experiments in space.

MOTOR CAR

By the end of World War One, more motor cars were becoming available. Their engines were lighter than steam engines, and used fuel made from oil. The motor car and its new engine changed the world. Towns spread. Horses disappeared from the streets, and motorized buses carried people on long and short trips. The tractor revolutionized agriculture. There are now over 450 million cars worldwide, causing congestion in cities and producing harmful air pollution which may contribute to global warming.

This car is a Volkswagen Beetle. Over 20 million have been produced, more than any other type of car. *Volkswagen* is German for "people's car".

SHRINKING PLANET

Since powered flight began in 1903, the twentieth century has seen tremendous developments in flight technology. Planes transformed warfare. Bombers destroyed cities and battles raged in the skies. Military inventions, such as the faster jet engine, were used in peacetime too. Jet engines revolutionized travel in the 1950s. International air travel has become much cheaper. Now the planet seems to have shrunk, as millions of people take flights across continents each year for work or leisure. In 1976 Concorde became the first passenger plane to fly faster than the speed of sound. Computer technology now helps pilots to fly planes even more safely.

SPACE

In 1957, the Soviets launched the first object into space – Sputnik, an information-gathering satellite. The superpowers competed for the glory of conquering space. A Soviet astronaut, Yuri Gagarin, was the first person in space in 1961, but eight years later, an American, Neil Armstrong, first walked on the Moon. Since the end of the Cold War, space technology around the world has been shared for exploration and communications. Now space probes are visiting distant planets to gather information.

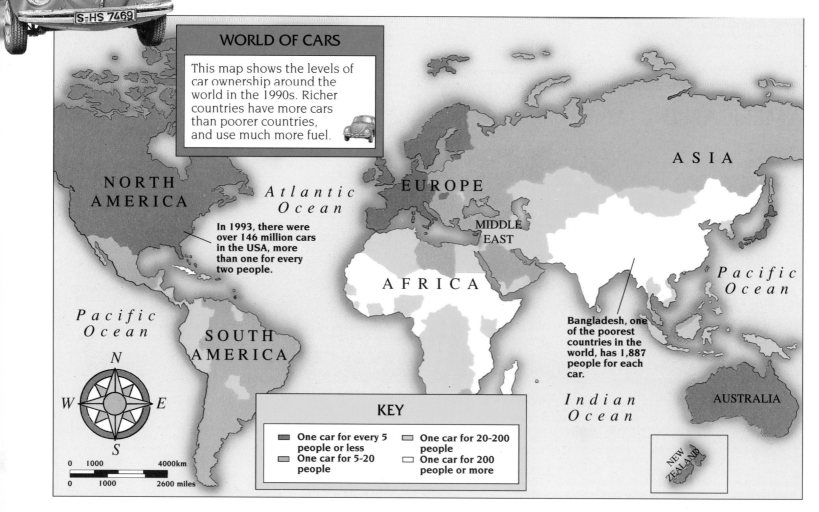

WORLD OF CARS

This map shows the levels of car ownership around the world in the 1990s. Richer countries have more cars than poorer countries, and use much more fuel.

NORTH AMERICA

Atlantic Ocean

EUROPE

ASIA

In 1993, there were over 146 million cars in the USA, more than one for every two people.

MIDDLE EAST

Pacific Ocean

AFRICA

Pacific Ocean

Bangladesh, one of the poorest countries in the world, has 1,887 people for each car.

Indian Ocean

AUSTRALIA

Pacific Ocean

SOUTH AMERICA

NEW ZEALAND

N W E S

0   1000   4000km
0   1000   2600 miles

KEY

■ One car for every 5 people or less
■ One car for 5-20 people
□ One car for 20-200 people
□ One car for 200 people or more

The American space shuttle made its first space flight in 1981. Unlike a rocket, it can be launched more than once.

Rocket engines power the shuttle in space. Its streamlined shape helps it to glide safely back to Earth.

COMMUNICATION

Before the twentieth century, people found out what was happening in other places from letters and newspapers. Now we can receive the news as it happens. First radio, then television and now solar-powered satellites started to transmit news directly into our homes. International telephone calls, once extremely expensive, are growing cheaper as optical cables below the Earth's surface each carry hundreds of thousands of calls and fax messages from one continent to another.

COMPUTER REVOLUTION

The first computers, built around the time of World War Two, were huge and slow. Since then, they have become smaller, cheaper and far more powerful. Computers, which store and process huge amounts of information, have transformed work in schools, offices and factories. Computerized robots can be programmed to do repetitive or dangerous tasks. All around the world, people can communicate with each other on the Internet, a giant computer network linked up using telephone lines.

FACT BOX

RENEWABLE ENERGY

As the world's population grows, so does the demand for energy. Traditional "fossil fuels" such as coal and oil will one day be used up, and they give off pollution when burned. Instead, we must develop clean and renewable energy from sources such as the wind or the sun which will not run out. Some of these are described below.

WIND POWER

"Wind farms" built on hillsides or by the coast use the endless, free energy from the wind. Each wind turbine has giant sails which are turned by the wind to generate electricity.

SOLAR ENERGY

The sun's energy can be harnessed using solar panels made of silicon. These absorb light and heat from the sun's rays, and can store the energy until it is needed.

METHANE OR BIOGAS

Methane is a "biogas", or natural gas given off by rotting waste. Millions of homes in the developing world have concrete-lined tanks buried in the ground to collect human and animal waste. The biogas produced is used for cooking or heating.

MEDICINE

In the 1940s antibiotics, such as penicillin, came into use. Made from microscopic fungus, they stop the spread of bacteria. This made surgery much safer, and so did better painkillers, blood transfusions and X-rays. By the 1960s, surgeons could replace faulty organs such as kidneys with others from donors. Scientists tackle new challenges all the time, such as finding a cure for Aids, and developing artificial hearts and other organs.

Medicines are now produced industrially, and are much cheaper. But they are still unavailable to many in the developing world. Weakened by lack of food, millions of children die there each year from diseases which could be prevented or cured with cheap, simple medical care.

Nigerian children waiting to be vaccinated against illness. Diseases such as smallpox have disappeared as a result of vaccination.

In this 1950s advertisement, a family shows off its new electric refrigerator.

ENERGY

New forms of energy became available in the twentieth century. By the 1930s, electricity powered an amazing variety of machines in the home and workplace. The first electricity generators burned coal, but later oil and gas were also used. Gradually, oil took over from coal as the major fuel. Regions rich in oil, such as the Middle East, grew in importance. Cheaper nuclear-generated electricity has been available since the 1950s, but it brings dangers such as the explosion at Chernobyl in 1986. In the twenty-first century, we will need to develop new environment-friendly energy sources.

THE CENTURY ENDS

The last ten years of the twentieth century started in a spirit of hope. Peace talks were set up to tackle complex and bitter conflicts in Israel and South Africa. The threat of nuclear destruction faded. Governments took positive steps to protect the environment.

This ballot paper is from South Africa's first multiracial elections. It uses pictures and symbols to make sure all voters know who they are voting for.

POLITICAL CHANGE

Fifty years of rivalry between the superpowers melted away as the Soviet Union broke up. International conflicts have subsided. But peace is hard to maintain. Many bitter civil wars still fester within countries around the world. Terrorists from various extremist groups have bombed planes and other targets to get their message across.

NEW FORCES

In some areas, especially in some of the old communist nations, the quest for self-rule turned into a fanatical desire for unity and hatred of outsiders. Yugoslavia, a country which contained many different peoples, started to split up in 1990. A terrible civil war followed, and in regions such as Bosnia, minority groups were forced to leave their homes to create areas which were purely Christian or Muslim. This sinister process was known as "ethnic cleansing".

WORLD NEGOTIATIONS

Since the end of the Cold War, there has been a growing spirit of trust between countries. The United Nations, still the main organization for negotiation between nations, has achieved a great deal, especially in its work with children, refugees and on health issues. But while its peacekeeping troops try to stop the worst of the bloodshed in civil wars, its powers to get involved in internal conflicts are very limited. Non-political groups such as Oxfam can bring international pressure, for instance to ban the use of landmines (tiny buried bombs which make land uninhabitable even after a war ends). Governments are sharing information to combat the terrorist threat.

SOUTH AFRICA

South Africa has at last dismantled apartheid. In 1990 the black leader, Nelson Mandela, was freed after 27 years in prison for his beliefs. He was elected president in the first multiracial elections in 1994. The new government faces huge challenges – to provide education, employment and health care for everyone denied it under apartheid.

THE WORLD TODAY

This map shows all the nations of the world at the end of the twentieth century. Throughout the century, borders shifted. Many new nations have won self-rule, often restoring ancient national territories.

GREENLAND
(DENMARK)

ALASKA
(USA)

CANADA

Atlantic
Ocean

UNITED STATES
OF AMERICA

Pacific
Ocean

HAWAII
(USA)

Throughout the century, millions of refugees have fled war or famine. Most go to countries nearby. Many countries in the West are now closing their doors to them.

BAHAMAS
CUBA
HAITI
DOMINICAN REPUBLIC
BELIZE
HONDURAS
JAMAICA
NICARAGUA
COSTA RICA
PANAMA
BARBADOS
TRINIDAD & TOBAGO
VENEZUELA
COLOMBIA
FRENCH GUIANA
ECUADOR

MEXICO

N
W   E
S

0   1000   2000 km
0   1000   miles

PERU
BRAZIL
BOLIVIA
PARAGUAY
CHILE
URUGUAY
ARGENTINA

Most Latin American countries are now democracies. Some are unstable.

Here Nelson Mandela (left), South Africa's first black prime minister, wears the team strip as he congratulates the nation's rugby captain on winning the World Cup. For decades, South Africa was banned from international sports

ENVIRONMENT

The Earth's growing population needs more food and fuel. But many new industry and farming methods harm the environment. Rainforests are being cut down, and the rising number of cars causes air pollution. As a result, the Earth's protective ozone layer is shrinking, and the climate is heating up, known as global warming. More land is turning into desert, increasing the risk of famine in poor countries. In 1992, at the Earth Summit conference, world leaders agreed on steps to tackle these threats, such as banning harmful chemicals. Global teamwork is vital to protect our environment in the twenty-first century.

An area in Indonesia where rainforest has been cleared for timber. Without trees, soil is easily blown or washed away, and land can become barren.

SHIFT TO THE EAST

Europe and the USA are no longer the world's only great industrial regions. Instead, production is shifting to the east. Japan and other Asian nations on the Pacific coast lead the world's high-tech industry. They export cars, computers and electrical goods around the world. Australia and New Zealand are turning now to these countries for trade instead of their traditional markets in Europe and the USA.

The countries of Europe are drawing still closer within the European Union. One day they may use a single currency.

Newly industrialized nations in Asia, such as Thailand, are known as "tiger economies", because they are so fiercely ambitious and successful.

Countries around the Pacific Ocean have formed trading alliances. Europe and the USA are no longer their main trading partners.

Having achieved independence within the last half of the twentieth century, many developing countries in Africa and Asia are still very poor. There is a long way to go before the inequality between rich and poor countries is ended.

In Rwanda, in central Africa, the Hutus and Tutsis fought a bloody civil war in 1994. These two groups were thrown together in one nation by the colonial powers. In 1996 conflict spread to nearby Burundi.

Map labels

ICELAND, NORWAY, SWEDEN, FINLAND, BRITAIN, IRELAND, DENMARK, ESTONIA, LATVIA, LITHUANIA, BELORUSSIA, GERMANY, POLAND, FRANCE, AUSTRIA, HUNGARY, ROMANIA, ITALY, UKRAINE, RUSSIAN FEDERATION, KAZAKHSTAN, MONGOLIA, N. KOREA, S. KOREA, JAPAN, Black Sea, Caspian Sea, TURKEY, GREECE, CYPRUS, SYRIA, IRAQ, IRAN, UZBEKISTAN, TURKMENISTAN, AFGHANISTAN, PAKISTAN, CHINA, Pacific Ocean, TAIWAN, PHILIPPINES, ISRAEL, JORDAN, KUWAIT, SAUDI ARABIA, OMAN, YEMEN, NEPAL, INDIA, BURMA (MYANMAR), LAOS, VIETNAM, THAILAND, PORTUGAL, SPAIN, Mediterranean Sea, TUNISIA, MOROCCO, ALGERIA, LIBYA, EGYPT, MAURITANIA, MALI, NIGER, CHAD, SUDAN, ERITREA, ETHIOPIA, SOMALIA, SENEGAL, GUINEA, IVORY COAST, GHANA, NIGERIA, CAMEROON, CENTRAL AFRICAN REPUBLIC, LIBERIA, GABON, CONGO, ZAIRE, RWANDA, KENYA, TANZANIA, ANGOLA, ZAMBIA, ZIMBABWE, NAMIBIA, BOTSWANA, MOZAMBIQUE, MADAGASCAR, SOUTH AFRICA, Indian Ocean, SEYCHELLES, MALDIVES, SRI LANKA, MAURITIUS, MALAYSIA, INDONESIA, BRUNEI, MICRONESIA, PALAU, MARSHALL ISLANDS, NAURU, KIRIBATI, PAPUA NEW GUINEA, SOLOMON ISLANDS, TUVALU, WESTERN SAMOA, VANUATU, FIJI, TONGA, AUSTRALIA, NEW ZEALAND, TASMANIA (AUSTRALIA)

LOOKING AHEAD

The twentieth century has brought unimaginable advances in democracy, science and industry. New technology is developing so fast that it is hard to predict how people will live in the new century. But progress has not closed the gap between rich and poor countries. Nearly a fifth of the world's people have too little to eat, and millions cannot read or write. Around the world, people are campaigning for a safer and more economic use of resources, so that everyone has the chance of a better and fairer life.

FIND OUT MORE

Apartheid	34
Developing countries	44
European Union	47

See above pages for more information.

GLOSSARY

Below is a list of important words used in this book. Words printed in bold type within a definition have their own separate entry.

aid Money or help given by one country to another that is poor or struck by disaster.

Allies The countries on the same side as Britain in the two world wars, including France and the USA.

ally An individual, group or country that gives help and support. An alliance is an agreement to support one another.

annex To occupy an area that was previously independent or under control of another country.

anti-Semitism Hatred and persecution of Jews.

apartheid The South African policy of keeping the different races apart, and not allowing nonwhite people the same rights as whites. The system was finally dismantled in 1994 by F. W. de Klerk and Nelson Mandela.

armistice An agreement between enemies at war to cease fighting and discuss peace terms.

assassination Murder, usually of someone famous or politically important.

atomic energy See **nuclear energy**.

Axis Powers The countries on the same side as Germany in World War Two, including Italy.

Bolshevik Originally a Russian **communist** and supporter of Lenin, working in order to cause revolution against the Czar of Russia. Later used as a general term to describe a communist.

capitalism An economic system, based on the private ownership of businesses and industry. Firms operate to make profit, and become efficient through competition.

Christianity The faith based on the teachings of Jesus Christ, set out in the New Testament. Christians believe Jesus is the son of God.

civil rights The rights of a citizen to personal freedom, including the right to vote, and legal and racial equality. The Civil Rights Movement campaigned for black people to have equal rights with whites in the USA in the 1960s.

civil war Fighting between rival groups or civilians within the same country.

cold war A struggle for power by all means short of fighting. The term is usually used to describe the struggle for supremacy in the 1950s and 60s between the **superpowers,** the USA and the Soviet Union.

colony An area and its people ruled from another country. For instance, Nigeria was a British colony until its **independence** in 1960.

communism A political system based on Karl Marx's writings, where the state owns all land and factories, and provides for people's needs. In the late 1980s, many countries in Eastern Europe rejected communism. China is now the world's largest communist country.

constitution The laws or political principles on which a state is ruled or governed.

constitutional monarchy A system of government by which a king or queen is head of state, but has no direct role in the decision-making of the government.

coup When one group uses force to take control of government away from another group.

culture The shared ideas, beliefs, values and traditions of a group of people.

Czar (or **tsar**) The Russian name for "Emperor". The word is a Slavonic form of the Latin "Caesar".

democracy A system of government where people can vote to elect representatives in the parliament or other governing body. There may be a **monarch**, but he or she has little real **constitutional** power. In Britain, for instance, the monarch is head of state but cannot overrule the elected government.

depose To remove someone (for instance a **dictator**) from power.

détente An improvement of relations between different nations, after a period of tension.

developing countries Countries, mostly in the southern hemisphere, that have not yet developed their full economic or industrial potential, often as a result of slavery or colonialism. Many are dependent on **aid** from richer nations.

dictator A ruler whose word is law, imposed by military force. Dictators often rule alone without the advice of a government.

economy The financial structure made up of all goods and services produced, sold and bought in a specific country or region.

election The selection by voting of a person or party to a position of power.

empire A large area of land, and its peoples, ruled by one powerful person or government. An example is the British Empire, which was at its height in the nineteenth century under Queen Victoria.

environment The surroundings in which humans, plants and animals live.

European Community An organization of European nations, originally formed for trade and **economic** purposes, but increasingly sharing financial, social and legal aims. Formerly known as the Common Market and now also known as the European Union.

Fascism The military form of government in Italy between 1922-43, led by the **dictator** Benito Mussolini, which was driven by **nationalism** and hostility to **communism**. The Fascists aimed to unify the country and, in an attempt to give it **economic** and military strength, put down all opposition. The name is also used for people or parties with similar views in other countries, such as Hitler's Germany.

feminism The movement that grew in the 1960s and 70s, campaigning for equal rights for women.

fundamentalism The strict following of a set of religious beliefs. In Christianity, it is the belief that the Bible is the source of all wisdom. In Islam, it is the strict observance of the teachings of the Ko'ran.

glasnost The Russian name for the policy of openness introduced in the **Soviet Union** in 1987 by Mikhail Gorbachev.

global warming The slow warming of the Earth's atmosphere, which is widely believed to be happening. It is thought to be caused by damage to the Earth's atmosphere, which in turn is caused by harmful gases (such as carbon dioxide) produced by industries and car exhausts.

Great Depression The period of worldwide unemployment and poverty, after the Wall Street Crash of 1929. The world's economy did not recover until the late 1930s.

guerillas A small band of fighters in combat with a larger army. Guerilla soldiers often fight for their strong political beliefs.

Hinduism The major faith in India. Hindus believe in reincarnation (rebirth in another form) and pray to many gods and goddesses. The Hindu caste system rigidly ranks groups in society according to their "purity" or importance, but the system is gradually losing its hold.

Holocaust The systematic murder of six million Jews by Nazi Germany between 1940 and 1945.

independence Self-rule, especially when it is achieved after a nation has been ruled by a foreign power. Many African and Asian countries achieved their independence after World War Two.

indigenous people The original inhabitants of a region. For example, the Aborigines of Australia or the Maoris of New Zealand are indigenous peoples.

inflation The rate of increase in prices of goods and services over a period of time.

Islam The religion of **Muslims**. Islam is based on the Ko'ran, the holy book which sets out the word of Allah (God) as revealed to prophet Muhammad (AD570-632).

isolationism A policy of non-participation in foreign affairs. The USA has followed this policy over several periods in its history, especially after World War One.

Judaism The religion of the Jews, based on worship of one God whose word is set down in the Torah (the first five books of the Old Testament). Jews do not worship Jesus, and believe the messiah (who will save the souls of humankind) has yet to come.

Kaiser The German name for "Emperor". The word comes from the Latin, "Caesar", after Julius Caesar.

majority rule Government by those who are politically or racially the same as most of their subjects.

mandates Former Axis colonies that the League of Nations put under control of one or other of the Allies, until they could be given independence. The term also means an official instruction.

Marxism Political theories following the teachings of Karl Marx (1818-83), that **communism** will overcome **capitalism**.

Middle East The Arabic-speaking region to the east of the Mediterranean Sea, and also including Turkey, Cyprus, Iran and most of North Africa.

monarch The head of state (king or queen) who inherits the crown. Few monarchs now have real power. The ruling of the state is entrusted to its government.

Muslim Someone who follows the faith of **Islam**.

nationalism The feeling of a common bond among people in a region who share a **culture**, language, history or religion. Nationalism often leads people to strive for unity and self-government.

natural resources Useful naturally-occurring materials, such as minerals, forests, fertile land, rivers and seas.

Nazism The **fascist** National Socialist movement in Germany, which grew out of the economic depression after World War One. In the 1920s and 30s, the Nazi Party was led by Adolf Hitler, whose policies caused World War Two to break out. The Nazis' fanatical **anti-Semitism** was also the cause of the **Holocaust**.

nuclear or atomic energy Energy created by splitting atoms. This releases a vast amount of energy which can be used in nuclear weapons or to make electricity.

pacifism The belief that all war is wrong, for whatever reasons. Pacifists believe that international tensions should be resolved by negotiation, not violence.

parliament An assembly of representatives, which meets for decision-making and law-giving.

perestroika The policies of restructuring and economic change in the Soviet Union which were begun in the 1980s under President Mikhail Gorbachev.

propaganda The organized distribution of information, such as on TV or in newspapers, in order to shape public opinion and discredit opposition.

protectorate A territory largely controlled by, but not **annexed** to, a more powerful nation.

rainforest Evergreen tropical forest, with very heavy rainfall, rich in plant and animal life. Rainforests, which are mainly in the southern hemisphere, contribute to global production of oxygen. Many are under threat from development for commercial purposes.

referendum A vote in which the electorate decides on an important single issue. For instance, some countries in Europe have had referendums on whether or not to agree to more controls under the **European Community**.

refugee Someone who flees from his or her home or country to seek safety. As well as from war or disaster, refugees flee from death threats or imprisonment for their beliefs.

republic A state where the people vote for their government in an **election**. A republic has no king or queen.

revolution The overthrow of a **monarch** or a government by mass action by the people.

revolutionaries People who try to cause revolutions or take part in them.

Russian Federation A state formed in 1992 from the alliance between Russia and parts of the old Soviet Union which now have self-rule.

Sikhism is based on the teachings of Guru Nanak. At their temple or *gurdwara*, Sikhs pray to one God and share food as a symbol of equality. All Sikhs share the surnames *Singh* for men and *Kaur* for women. Sikhs are campaigning for an independent homeland in northern India.

socialism A political system whereby every member of society has equal rights, all factories and farms are run by and for the people, and wealth is distributed equally between them.

Soviet Union The name given to the communist state formed in 1922 after the Russian Revolution of 1917. Also known as the USSR. It stretched from Eastern Europe to Asia. It broke up in 1991, when many of its republics gained independence.

suffragettes Women who campaigned for suffrage (the right to vote) at the end of the nineteenth and the beginning of the twentieth century. Suffragettes drew attention to their cause by getting arrested and going on hunger strike in prison.

superpower A very powerful state. The term is usually applied to the USA or the former **Soviet Union**.

terrorism Bomb attacks or other threats of violence used by extremist groups to try to force governments to meet their demands.

trade union An association of employees who band together in order to improve their pay and working conditions.

treaty A formal agreement between countries, usually relating to peace, trade or becoming **allies**.

unemployment Having no job and therefore not being able to earn money for oneself or one's dependents.

United Nations An international organization of independent states which aims to promote understanding and peace between nations of the world.

The West The capitalist countries of Western Europe and North America.

Zionism Political movement which campaigned for a Jewish homeland in Palestine.

MAP INDEX

This index lists all the place names shown on the maps. As well as page numbers, it gives the country or region for each place and alternative names through history, for example: Constantinople (now Istanbul).

A

Abu Dhabi United Arab Emirates 30
Adelaide Australia 51
Aden Protectorate (now part of Yemen)
    Middle East 13, 30
Adriatic Sea Europe 6, 26
Aegean Sea Europe 8
Afghanistan Asia 32, 55
Africa 4, 12, 19, 20, 24, 34, 45, 49, 52, 55
Agadir Morocco 4
Alaska USA 54
Albania Europe 5, 39, 46, 55
Albert France 7
Algeria Africa 4, 24, 30, 34, 35, 55
Algiers Algeria 24, 30
Amman Jordan 13, 30
Andorra Europe 55
Angola Africa 35, 55
Ankara Turkey 13
Antigua and Barbuda Central America 54
ANZAC Cove Turkey 8
Arabia 8, 19
Aral Sea 20, 46
Archangel Russia 10
Arctic Ocean 10, 20, 38, 46
Argentina South America 36, 37, 54
Armenia Europe 46, 55
Asia 20, 24, 25, 27, 32, 34, 45, 46, 49, 52, 55
Asia Minor 43
Astrakhan Russia 10
Asuncion Paraguay 36
Atlanta USA 14, 50
Atlantic Ocean 4, 14, 24, 38, 45, 46, 48, 51, 52, 54
Auckland New Zealand 51
Australia 33, 45, 49, 51, 52, 55
Austria Europe 12, 19, 22, 28, 29, 46, 47, 55
Austro-Hungarian Empire Europe 5, 6, 8
Azerbaijan Europe 46, 55
Azores *islands* Atlantic Ocean 38

B

Baghdad Iraq 13, 30
Bahamas Central America 54
Bahrain Middle East 55
Baku Azerbaijan 10
Baltic Sea Europe 10, 19, 25, 29, 46
Baltimore USA 14
Bangkok Thailand 33
Bangladesh (was East Pakistan) Asia 32, 33, 40, 44, 55
Bapaume France 7
Barbados Central America 54
Bayeux France 26
Bechuanaland (now Botswana) Africa 34
Beijing China 17, 33, 40, 41
Beirut Lebanon 13, 30, 42, 43
Belarus Europe 46, 55
Belgium Europe 6, 7, 22, 23, 28, 46, 47, 55
Belize Central America 36, 54
Belmopan Belize 36
Bengal India/Bangladesh 44
Benghazi Libya 24
Benin Africa 35, 55
Berlin Germany 22, 27, 28, 29, 39, 47
Bethlehem Israel 42
Bhutan Asia 16, 32, 33, 40, 44, 55
Black Sea Europe 10, 12, 13, 19, 20, 29, 46, 55
Bogota Colombia 36
Bolivia South America 36, 54
Bonn Germany 47
Bosnia-Herzegovina Europe 5, 6, 46, 55

Boston USA 14
Botswana (was Bechuanaland) Africa 34, 35, 55
Brasilia Brazil 36
Bratislava Slovakia 47
Brazil South America 36, 37, 54
Brest-Litovsk Belarus 10
Brisbane Australia 51
Britain Europe 6, 7, 12, 19, 23, 26, 28, 37, 46, 50, 55
Brno Czech Republic 47
Brunei Asia 33, 55
Bucharest Romania 47
Buenos Aires Argentina 36
Bulgaria Europe 5, 8, 19, 27, 29, 39, 46, 47, 55
Burkina Faso Africa 35, 55
Burma (Myanmar) Asia 16, 32, 33, 40, 44, 55
Burundi Africa 35

C

Cabinda Africa 55
Caen France 26
Cairo Egypt 13, 30
Cambodia (was part of French Indochina) Asia 33, 55
Cameroon (was Cameroons) Africa 12, 35, 55
Cameroons (now Cameroon) Africa 12
Canada North America 14, 38, 46, 48, 51, 54
Çanakkale Turkey 8
Canberra Australia 51
Canton (now Guangzhou) China 16, 17
Cape Helles Turkey 8
Cape Horn South America 36
Caracas Venezuela 36
Carentan France 26
Caribbean Sea Central America 14, 39
Caspian Sea Europe/Asia 10, 13, 20, 43, 46, 55
Cayenne French Guiana 36
Central African Republic Africa 35, 55
Central America 36
Ceylon (now Sri Lanka) Asia 32
Chad Africa 35, 55
Chengdu China 40, 41
Chicago USA 14
Chile South America 36, 54
China Asia 5, 16, 17, 21, 32, 33, 38, 39, 40, 41, 44, 45, 49, 54
Cleveland USA 14
Cologne Germany 28
Colombia Central America 36, 54
Colombo Sri Lanka 33, 44
Comoros Africa 35, 55
Congo Africa 35, 55
Congo *river* Africa 4
Constantinople (now Istanbul) Turkey 5, 10, 13
Cooper's Creek *river* Australia 51
Coral Sea *battle* Pacific Ocean 25
Costa Rica Central America 36, 54
Coventry Britain 28
Croatia Europe 46, 55
Cuba Central America 14, 38, 39, 54
Cyprus Middle East 13, 55
Cyrenaica *region* Libya 23
Czechoslovakia (now Czech Republic and Slovakia)
    Europe 12, 19, 22, 28, 29, 47
Czech Republic (see also Czechoslovakia) Europe
    46, 47, 55

D

Dalstrop *region* Russia 21
Damascus Syria 8, 13, 30, 42
Danzig (now Gdansk) Poland 22

Dardanelles *strait* Turkey 8
Denmark Europe 9, 46, 55
De Panne Belgium 23
Detroit USA 14
Dhaka Bangladesh 33
Djibouti Africa 35, 55
Dominica Central America 54
Dominican Republic Central America 57
Dresden Germany 28
Dunkirk France 23
Dutch East Indies (now Indonesia) 32

E

East China Sea Asia 40
East Germany (now part of Germany) Europe 29, 39, 47
East Pakistan (now Bangladesh) 32
East Prussia (former German territory) Europe 22
Ecuador South America 36, 54
Egypt Africa 13, 24, 30, 31, 34, 35, 42, 43, 55
El Alamein *battle* Egypt 24
El Salvador Central America 36, 54
English Channel Europe 23, 26
Equatorial Guinea Africa 35, 55
Eritrea Africa 35
Essen Germany 28
Estonia Europe 12, 46, 55
Ethiopia Africa 19, 35, 55
Euphrates *river* 13
Europe 9, 20, 24, 28-29, 45, 46, 49, 52, 55
    Eastern Europe and Western Europe 38
Eyre, Lake Australia 51

F

Falkland Islands South Atlantic Ocean 36, 37
Fiji Pacific Ocean 55
Finland Europe 8, 12, 19, 46, 54
Formosa (now Taiwan) Asia 16
France Europe 6, 7, 12, 19, 23, 26, 28, 29, 46, 47, 55
Frankfurt Germany 28
French Guiana South America 36, 54
French Indochina (now Laos, Vietnam and Cambodia)
    Asia 16

G

Gabon Africa 35, 55
Galapagos Islands Pacific Ocean 36
Gallipoli Turkey 8
Gambia Africa 35, 55
Gdansk (was Danzig) Poland 22, 47
Georgetown Guyana 36
Georgia Europe 46, 55
German East Africa Africa 12
German Southwest Africa (now Namibia) Africa 4, 12
Germany Europe (see also East Germany and West
    Germany) 6, 8, 12, 19, 22, 23, 25, 27, 28, 46, 47,
    54
Ghana Africa 35, 55
Golan Heights *region* Syria 42
Great Lakes USA/Canada 14
Great Sandy Desert Australia 51
Greece Europe 5, 8, 19, 29, 38, 46, 55
Greenland *island* Atlantic Ocean 38, 45, 46, 54
Grenada Central America 54
Guam *island* Pacific Ocean 38
Guangzhou (was Canton) China 16, 17, 40
Guatemala Central America 36, 38, 54
Guatemala City Guatemala 36
Guinea Africa 35, 55

MAP INDEX

INDEX

Main entries for subjects are shown in bold type.

INDEX

INDEX

LINE FOR
1¢ RESTAURANT

20 MEALS FOR 1¢

DONATIONS WANTED
HELP FEED THE HUNGRY
I WILL FEED 20
1¢ RESTAURANT
107 W 43ᴿᴰ ST

ACKNOWLEDGMENTS

The publishers would like to thank the
following for permission to use their
photographs in this book:

AKG London (28 left, 29 bottom);
Arhivo Fotografico Oronoz (19);
Associated Press/Topham (41 bottom);
Corbis UK (50 bottom); David King
Collection (38 left, 41 middle, 47 left);
Hulton Getty (9, 10, 12, 13, 16, 18, 21, 22
bottom, 24 bottom, 25, 26, 28 right, 30,
32, 34 right, 37 top, 41 top, 52); Imperial
War Museum (34 left, 48 top right); Sir
David Low/Evening Standard/Cartoon
Study Centre, University of Kent,
Canterbury (22 middle bottom); Mrs. P.
Miles (22 top; 23); Panos Pictures (37
bottom; 44, 45, 55); Popperfoto (cover,
5, 8, 22 middle top, 24 top, 31, 42
bottom, 43, 46, 47 right, 48 top left, 48
bottom, 50 top, 54); Topham
Picturepoint (15, 29 top; 39, 42 top, 53
top, 53 bottom).

Additional illustrations by:
Philip Argent, Andrew Beckett, Andy Burton,
Peter Dennis, Nicholas Hewetson, Janos
Marffy, Radhi Parekh, Qui Kai Jun
and Ross Watton.

Figures for the map on car ownership on
page 52 is based on *World Road Statistics* supplied by
the International Road Federation, Geneva.

Every effort has been made to trace and
acknowledge ownership of copyright.
The publishers will be glad to make suitable
arrangements with any copyright holder whom it
has not been possible to contact.